THE TAME OX

THE TAME OX

STORIES BY

JACK COPE

HEINEMANN

LONDON MELBOURNE TORONTO

William Heinemann Ltd
LONDON MELBOURNE TORONTO
CAPE TOWN AUCKLAND
THE HAGUE

First published 1960

Printed in Great Britain
by The Windmill Press Ltd
Kingswood, Surrey

CONTENTS

ACKNOWLEDGMENTS

Some of these stories first appeared in the following publications: *London Magazine, John Bull, Paris Review, Cape Argus, Standpunte, Harper's Magazine, English Studies in South Africa, Cape Times, Pick of Today's Short Stories, Faber Book of South African Short Stories, Argosy.*

THE TAME OX

The College secretary, the Reverend Charles Gumede, stood at the door of the Principal's office, smiling pleasantly, his teeth brilliantly white and his eyes twinkling behind glasses.

'More people to see you, Chief, many more.'

The Principal stood up, breathing in his thick, heavy way, and glanced at his watch. He was a big man, tall and long in the arm, and had the shoulders of a lion.

'I'll come out, Charles,' he said; 'I think I should stay out.'

'Yes, Chief. They are coming fast now. There's going to be a big crowd, very big – a great day.' He spoke smoothly, rolling his words, but was inwardly excited.

'I'll wear my gown, I think.'

The secretary helped his chief on with his academic robe and the two Zulus stood back, glancing at each other. In the big man's eyes was an affectionate glow; they were large, rather protruding eyes that enveloped all about him with a generous dignified sweep.

'I ate too much lunch,' the Principal said, buttoning his frock-coat and smoothing down the wrinkles. 'Go on ahead, Charles, I'll follow.' They came out on the veranda and the Principal rested his hands on the railing.

A sing-song of greeting voices rose up and tingled in his ears. He smiled and waved. The newcomers were women, Christians in simple chaste cotton dresses down to the ankles. Their feet were bare and their heads were covered with black and red cloths or knitted caps.

7

'It's going to be a big day indeed. I won't guess how many people are coming,' Reverend Gumede repeated.

The Principal lowered his eyes. His heart was beating in exultation, only he would not like to show pride to Charles, the clever, unassuming Charles.

'The Europeans will be here before long,' Gumede continued, looking involuntarily into the distance where the road wound up the valley towards St Cyprian's Mission College.

'No, Charles – give them another hour and more. Miss Poynton will be here at three, and she's always first.'

The veranda of the office looked across a square of low roofs, and beyond them other buildings of the Native College could be seen scattered among the wind-swept gum trees, one- and two-storey blocks in plain stone masonry topped with corrugated iron. Beyond the campus again stretched rolling hills of sugar-cane plantations. The College Principal, the Reverend Dr Luke Njilo, descended the steps to the broad red-earth square. Along the left side was a row of huge old mango trees. It was a tropical day of broiling sunshine and limp, hot air. The dust lay still and the flags round the platform were motionless. The mango trees had their feet in circles of deep shadow. By the time the ceremony was due to begin the platform would be mostly shaded.

Dr Njilo went among the people, moving his big body with an ease that was solemn but at the same time youthful. The women fixed on him coy, bashful looks and smiled. He was a great man, but distant from them. That day he was to be honoured by the white race. An honorary degree, a Doctorate of Philosophy – these were strange terms to them. Yet they knew no other man of the Zulu nation had ever before arrived where he had. The word had gone out and

8

the people were coming from long distances to see the white men do honour to the teacher, Luke Njilo.

Dr Njilo had a few words for all he greeted. He put into his own language an unusual preciseness, a stiffness of the printed letter and book as though he had a proprietary right but no pride in it. He turned to his secretary a few times with a remark in English. The women had brought beer in earthenware pots and large gourds covered with a few willow leaves. He could not refuse the customary offering. During the morning he had drunk a good deal and the midday meal had revived his thirst. At first he took the beer-pots from the Reverend Gumede's hands, drank a few gulps, standing, and then wiped his mouth with his handkerchief. There was little to indicate his pleasure or approval. Perhaps his eyes lit up if he came on a fine brew, but he silenced his belches in the European manner and merely nodded as if he were making a severe concession in accepting at all.

In the shade of the mango trees an old wrinkled woman, more pagan than Christian, remarked in a cracked voice: 'Teacher, if you stand, the beer has far to travel – it will make a waterfall.' The people turned their faces away to hide their smiles, but Dr Njilo burst into a hearty laugh in which all joined. 'A waterfall? Is that where the Amanzimtoti River started?' He had a resonant, bell-like voice.

Sitting on his haunches, he took a good pull at the old woman's beer-pot and handed it back with a compliment. He was speaking more easily; his quips flew, and now there was a ripple of amusement where the solid dark figure moved, clothed in academic robes. The sun flickered in patches between the leaves on his crisp black hair, neatly parted. He was sweating freely in the all-pervading heat and breathed like a strong-chested horse in the traces. His pro-

A*

truding eyes rolled amiably and a healthy pink tongue showed when he threw back his head to laugh.

At one place six elders were waiting for him, all grey-headed men. Some were in European clothes, others in the skins and sandals of tribal dress; one man, creased and dim-eyed with age, had on the polished head-ring of the old royal warriors. Dr Njilo did not know them – perhaps grand-fathers or great-uncles of students. There was a short awkward pause. They regarded him with the cool impassive bearing of men who are perfectly assured of their own place. The head of the eldest nodded continually and spittle dribbled over his beard. The others looked through dark, half-closed eyes, faintly contemptuous, it seemed. He had been criticised before; the extremists among his own people called him a 'good boy', a 'tame ox'. As editor of the weekly *People's Voice*, he was on the side of moderation, tolerance. He mixed with white missionaries, Negrophiles like Miss Poynton, liberals, and even men who galled him with their patronage. He glanced at Charles Gumede and back at the old men. They were not the kind to criticise him politically. But they were studying him, weighing up the future that he stood for as if gazing into the clouds to divine what storms or what sunny days were in store.

One of them casually threw him a greeting and he re-sponded to the ancient law of humility from a young man to his elders. 'My father, I see you well.' The women near-by and the students in badly-fitting best clothes saw the great teacher Njilo humble before these illiterate patriarchs. But the reserve faded. Soon they were speaking to him with animated faces and slow, expressive gestures. A pot of beer circulated among them and Dr Njilo took his turn. He wiped his lips as they did, with the palm of his hand.

'I'll be back in a moment,' he said to Reverend Gumede as he stood up. He climbed the steps and passed through the corridor of the office block. At some distance from the back of the building was a straggling row of thorny matingula shrubs, once a hedge, and behind them the tin roof of a privy. Dr Njilo made his way there and returned quickly. He could not endure the noisome stench of the earth closet, the drumming flies, and the heat. It was the only type of sanitation. Sanitation – what a word, he thought. Any sub-standard school for white children would have water-borne sewerage. But his College, his University, had to be content with this. Who was to benefit, after all? An ugly word came to his mind. Ah, they were lucky to have anything at all. He knew how requests were stalled with smooth or slighting remarks. It needed infinite patience and forbearance to shift forward a single peg of progress.

Dr Njilo paused in the comparative cool of the office corridor and ran his handkerchief round the inside of his collar. He let the air in under his gown and frock-coat. Feeling relaxed, he went on. The square was filling. On its open space under the mango trees to the left there were already nearly two thousand people. Some had spread straw mats and sat enjoying the fierce sun. A tumbling murmur of voices rose up; bright colours met his eye. The Principal wanted a space kept open in front of the platform; it was the only area grown with grass – not a lawn in the English sense, for it was tufty and rugged, but it was green and Miss Poynton thought it a beginning. The guests would be escorted straight to the platform for the capping ceremony, and afterwards a reception in the hall. He would like to call it the Great Hall, except that it was not great; it was a cement and iron shed.

The Chancellor of the University of South Africa would

be there. He was conferring the Honorary Degree of Ph.D. on Dr Njilo. He would wear his medieval cap and gold-faced gown, his hood lined with ermine and scarlet. And others: an academic representative from England and one from America, the principals of two white universities and members of their senate, the Bishop, government officials, and so on, and so on. Miss Poynton had seen to that. They would have a royal welcome – three or four thousand people. Dr Njilo felt light-hearted. He looked again at his watch and into the distance at the road approach. The air over the sugar-cane fields shimmered and the red ribbon of road seemed in the mirage to be under a sheet of glistening water. Another hour to go.

The College boys politely cleared the grass path and began to marshal the people into a wide mass about the platform. It would be like a great *indaba*, a people's council. At the centre would be the whites and he, Njilo – Luke the son of Nxaba, of the renowned Mukazi, of Macoco, nine generations back to Bahuza.

Dr Njilo was holding a beer-pot and smiled suddenly at the absurdity of this thought. They were not honouring a man for his barbarian ancestry recalled in a string of poetic 'praises' full of bloodshed and Homeric boasting. He was, that day, pre-eminently the successful product of the missionary, the philanthropist, and of British education in the humanities; the wisely moderate editor of an officially approved native newspaper and the moderately wise principal of a liberal native college, the tame ox, as his critics said.

He turned to Reverend Gumede: 'If I am a tame ox, what are you, Charles?'

Gumede did not relish the joke. There was a youthful and lovable sincerity about his face and the flash of pain that crossed it was visible. Deeply, seriously, he was attached to his chief. 'I try to be a servant of God,' he said mildly.

'Amen,' Reverend Njilo responded quickly, resting his eyes on his young friend.

'One must expect reproaches,' said Gumede.

For a short while Njilo was silent and downcast. Gumede and the people about looked anxiously at his face. But when he glanced up there was a play of mischief in his wide-set eyes. He took a draught at the beer-pot.

'Charles, I was thinking about my ancestors. What would they make of all this?'

'One is close to one's ancestors here,' the secretary said, nodding in the direction of the crowd.

'You are too serious and clever today. No, I was only picturing the old men, without conciliating any spirits. Who was this Bahuza? Nine generations before me in the line of chiefs – that would have him living earlier than the first white invaders, centuries before our people even brushed with them. And what does history say of him? "He killed Nomjoni at the water-hole like a crocodile . . ." That's all. A name and a phrase. I don't believe he ever existed, really, or else he's a mixture of memory and myth. Still, do you think anyone will compose a line about me being capped today?' He let out a guffaw of laughter and improvised a few 'praises' for himself in a ludicrous strain. The people were warming up to him. His words were passed round to surges of merriment.

'Charles, Miss Poynton will be here soon. Keep an eye open for her Cadillac.'

Dr Njilo went off back through the office block and out behind. As he neared the privy the stench met his nostrils. 'That thing!' he exclaimed aloud. 'Third-class – we travel through our world third-class.' He snorted and veered off stolidly towards the cane-field. There, near the first row of sugar cane, he took his ease. Through the gaps in the thorn trees he could see people coming up the road. The sun blazed hotly on him.

Walking down, he felt the heat in his face, and his clothes seemed rather close about him. He was quite firm on his legs though with slower movements than usual, and his boots felt tight. These were minor discomforts dispelled by the great glow that spread from his heart. As he entered the crowd again he was like a river among his native reeds. They chattered, swayed, and responded to his every movement. His big eyes turned in majestic glances from one face to another and he spoke to those he recognised, using their names and the names of their fathers. He had a passion for the wild valleys, rocky corn patches, and sweet-scented brakes of bush where his clan had clung against every misfortune for so many generations. He asked close questions about the grain baskets, the children and cattle, and the white-tailed rock hares he used to hunt as a boy. They answered in more glowing terms than the truth, telling him what he wanted to hear – that all was well.

Reverend Gumede intercepted him as he raised a beer-pot to his lips.

'Miss Poynton will expect to have tea with you, Chief . . . keep some space for that.' He smiled apologetically.

'Tea!' Dr Njilo gasped. Then he looked round with a merry chuckle. 'Tea! Do you hear that? Tea with Miss Poynton.' He made a gesture of delicately picking up a cup and arched his little finger. The women held their sides and shrilled out peals of laughter. Reverend Gumede watched in consternation. Then something saved him.

'Look! Here she comes.' He pointed.

Reverend Dr Njilo stood up and, leaning one hand heavily on his secretary's shoulder, shaded his eyes with the other.

'Yes,' he said. 'That's her. Come, Charles.'

He adjusted the gown round his shoulders. His mouth closed up firm and the short aquiline nose with flared nostrils was like the black beak of a Viking ship as he steered his way towards the lower end of the square. They passed the chapel and came out under the gum trees as the long cream-coloured Cadillac drew up. A Zulu chauffeur jumped out and opened the rear door for Miss Poynton, patroness of St Cyprian's College and heiress of a pioneer gold-mining millionaire.

'This is a great day, Luke,' she said, holding out her hand.

Dr Njilo took the podgy little fist and shook it without a word. His eyes were brimming, which she took for a sign of emotion. Dr Njilo did not underrate the humanity and generosity of Miss Poynton but he could not take her seriously. Constantly she said and did things that would have hurt his pride had he been looking for injury. To her own satisfaction she understood 'the Zulu mind'. It was an abstraction from the colonial histories, the novels of Rider Haggard, and the almost feudal loyalties between tribesmen and her family on one of her late father's Zululand labour estates. To her, Dr Luke Njilo was a prodigy and was, essentially, 'the Zulu mind' writ large. He was loyal, grateful, clean, dignified, a perfect gentleman. Because he was all these things he was capable of being a Christian and attaining great distinctions in learning. The decision of the governing university to confer on him its highest honour rounded off her work on Luke's behalf.

A class of girl students with radiant faces, white teeth and clear eyes against their dark features, presented Miss Poynton with a bouquet of wild flowers. Their brown skins were glossy and the flowers brought the colours and perfume of the valleys to set off Miss Poynton's grey hair and fluffy, middle-aged complexion. Dr Njilo wagged a finger at the students in mock seriousness. 'And who forgot to roll out the red carpet?' They giggled, shaking their shoulders comfortably.

The Principal drew Miss Poynton's arm through his. She shot him a startled glance. There was no mistake about his breath; his voice was slightly thick and his eyes reddened. But it was customary to drink a little beer on special occasions and 'the Zulu' could imbibe a gallon or two without much feeling the effect.

'Let me conduct you to the seat of honour,' he smiled – 'the seat of honour.'

'The others will be here directly. Shouldn't we wait for them?'

'They are here today and gone tomorrow. But to you we owe everything. Charles will keep a look-out.'

She held out a hand to Gumede. 'Charles, I'm delighted to see you . . I really would like to go and look everything over. I'm so thrilled, you don't know.'

Miss Poynton was broad-backed and short and could not avoid a waddle in her gait. Reverend Charles Gumede watched the two receding through the flickering shadows of the gum trees, the short white woman like an outhouse to the tower of the Principal in his black robe. He saw this as a communion of spirits, the forgetting of self for a common good. The wolf shall dwell with the lamb and the leopard shall lie down with the kid.

Hundreds of people were still streaming in from the

countryside. Along the paths they came and all one could see above the sugar cane of those more distant was bright-coloured hair-cloths or the pots of beer balanced gracefully on the women's heads. Here and there was the fur cap of an old man. Most of the young men were absent in the towns. Girls from the unbaptised villages, as a bow to the Christian occasion, had suspended on their bosoms a pocket handker-chief or a yellow flannel duster from which their dark coral-coloured nipples peeped.

Suddenly the hubbub of voices swelled. The cars were coming in sight in the distance under puffs of brown-red dust. Gumede was agitated. He did not feel confident of welcoming all the distinguished men about to descend on the Native College. Staff and students were bunching up to greet the visitors and he dispatched a student to summon the Principal. There was no formality, no guard of honour, as some of the College Governors had suggested. People thronged about cheerfully.

The messenger found Dr Njilo sitting on the platform edge deliberately taking off his boots. Miss Poynton, in her seat behind him, looked worried.

'Is there anything the matter, Luke?'

Dr Njilo wrenched the second boot off and threw it down with a grunt. 'Uncomfortable,' he said. Breathing heavily, he stripped off his socks as well and wriggled his toes. The student repeated his message for the third time. Turning to Miss Poynton, Dr Njilo said: 'The cars are here.' It was so casual. He might have been saying: 'Tea is served.' He took a few steps about to try his released feet. Then he sprang on to the platform and raised his hand. There was a hush.

'They have come!' he shouted.

'Ah,' responded the mass in a deep murmur.

'They have come from Cape Town and Pretoria, from England and America. I will not tell you what they have come for – you know.'

'We know,' rolled back the response. An elderly man stood up, raised a polished black-wood stick and began reciting Dr Luke Njilo's praises. There was a new one devised for the occasion – 'The beer-pots flowed over for him.' Dr Njilo gave an agile leap into the air and came down with a thud on the boards of the platform. Miss Poynton was on her feet and tapped him imperatively on the elbow. 'Luke, they are actually arriving.'

'Ah, let me go to meet them.' He bounded off the platform.

'Your boots!' she cried after him. But he was already hastening through the lanes of admiring faces towards the Chapel.

They met almost at the door of the Chapel. The Chancellor had Reverend Charles Gumede at his side and Dr Njilo came down alone. To the distinguished men who witnessed it the encounter was strangely moving, spontaneous. Holding the folds of his gown about him with one hand, the big Zulu hurried forward with a slight bow. The slender white-haired Englishman simply took both his shoulders in his grip and held him in silence. Then they shook hands. The Chancellor was affected to see the African scholar and churchman, the deserving recipient of high honours, come to him in such modesty with the dust on his bare feet. Together they proceeded to the square. Dr Njilo listened as if rapt to every word of the Chancellor, his head to one side and his breathing coming thick and regular.

'What a magnificent crowd,' said the visitor.

'They have come to see you, sir.'

'And to do honour to you, Dr Njilo.'

18

'But they are my family,' he laughed. 'I am a prophet in his own land.'

'Then you are the happy exception, not without honour.'

Cars were arriving every minute. Scores of white people followed the official party or edged for standing room in the shade of the mango trees. The Chief Native Commissioner, the Director of Education, and the Commandant of Police represented the State. The Bishop was there, academic dons, members of the joint councils and the race relations institute, Pressmen.

Miss Poynton met them on the platform. Standing there alone, she looked like a stout caryatid in grey stone, petrified with anxiety. The guests lined up before their chairs, flanked with motionless flags and overtopped by shining dark-green mango leaves. The whole mass of people stood up and from their throats swelled the nation's salute, starting from a low rumble of the men's voices and rising in a single short crescendo.

'Today we are proud but humble,' Dr Njilo shouted in Zulu. The crowd murmured as they sat down. 'Today is a day of victory!'

'*Ga-zi!*' came a muffled reply – Blood!

A grey-headed Zulu stood out near the corner of the platform and began a rhythmic oration in a high voice with a quick, pulsing tempo. He spoke of the honour done their son that day by great men of the world. The people could look for themselves and see who was before them – the right hand of the Government and eagles who had flown from far lands. These great men he welcomed. They came in peace and it was a victory of peace. He then spoke of Njilo and of the nation. He was the rain who would bring up good crops; he it was who watched the herds.

Dr Njilo could restrain himself no longer. He leaped down from the platform, his gown flying out like a huge black bird's wings. With quick, short steps he began to circle the turf area, clapping his hands and shouting random phrases as a warrior does when he throws out a challenge. From the back of the crowd a woman's voice started to shrill a trembling monotone. Another joined her and another, and the whole mass were drawn into a fast exciting song. Dr Njilo's feet thudded on the ground; he was dancing. Down the open space he went a second time and retreated to the platform with the springy movements of a leopard. As a thousand hands clapped a rhythm, he whirled into the *giya* dance with a stupendous leap; the war-dance of the Zulus. Round and round he sped, killing a thousand imaginary enemies, cursing wizards, hurling insults at the sky. At times forced almost to his knees in mock defeat, he rose again and the ceaseless beat of his feet carried him into a paroxysm of physical triumph.

The Bishop sat still, a withered smile on his kindly, intelligent face. The Commandant of Police was enjoying it in his own way: How right I am about these black devils, he thought. Miss Poynton looked like a guinea-fowl shot on the wing; she was rapidly coming to earth, her eyes stared before her in a piteous, dying expression. Her ideal of progress seemed in ruins, the feet of the idol crumbling away. Behind the platform Reverend Charles Gumede stood with closed eyes and his lips moved as if in prayer.

The Chancellor rose and advanced slowly to the front of the platform. His blue eyes sparkled; he was amazed but full of admiration. An old warrior chanted wildly: 'They say he is a tame ox. There he is, hau! hau! hau! a black-maned lion among the herds!' There was a tumult of joy.

The people threw shouted remarks at the dancer as he spun on his giddy round. Dr Njilo heard their words and they sank into his heart, braving him on. He wanted to do something prodigious – he was doing it. No man had ever before danced a *giya* in an academic gown and frock-coat. They got in his way, flapped round his legs and arms. But he had made men call him a lion. It was a deserved tribute. The *élan* of a tremendous physique flowed into his whole being. All other things came to him with the same strenuous ease: the mastery of learning, the understanding of nature, and the feeling for God. Men alone had seemed always to escape him. Today he had found them and he exulted.

Turning, he saw the curious row of white people on the platform. He stopped with a short, breathless laugh. There was in it a blend of pride and apology like a youth who has been caught in some meritorious but forbidden act. He was coming back to the sedate world of letters and religion – his world.

Dr Njilo pulled up the drooping gown about his shoulders and mopped his whole face, tucking the handkerchief back in his breast pocket. He was balanced on a knife-edge between bathos and disgust and he kept his balance. With light but firm steps he walked forward. His lungs pumped, deep and powerful, and his nostrils were wide. In those few moments his face took on its solid composure, a sober dignity.

The Chancellor reached down a hand. Dr Njilo took it and sprang up easily.

'I think they would expect it,' he said with an amicable gesture towards the crowd.

'They enjoyed it too, a most remarkable rendering of the dance.'

'I am afraid, sir, the trappings of civilisation were somewhat in the way.' He twitched his gown, now smiling blandly.

'Not at all, Dr Njilo,' said the Chancellor.

And the ceremony went on.

A CRACK IN THE SKY

They walked past the wind-pump and they both looked up at the slowly turning iron vanes. Beyond them, the sky was an iron blue, clear and so hard in the heat that it seemed it must crack like a plate. If the sky cracked, the boy wondered what he might see beyond. It was a terrifying and marvellous thought; the stars would come showering down in broad daylight, looking not white and cold but red-hot.

'Have you ever in your life seen a crack in the sky, Outa Flip?' he asked his companion.

Without thinking, the old coloured man answered: '*Ja, my basie*.' He shuffled on and the white boy walked at his side with his slight limp and his little pinched face looking as sharp and lively as a bird's. Old Flip then glanced up at the sky again past the wind-pump vanes and down at the trickle of water from the pipe into the open drinking-tank. It dawned on him what the boy had asked and he knew he was in for some stubborn questioning.

'So you have seen a crack – when?'

Flip said: 'Look now at that storm-bird. The way he's calling means rain.'

'Rain,' the boy echoed dully. 'No, it will never rain again.' From the fevered despair of his parents and the torment that lay over the land the word 'rain' troubled him. His excitement at the prospect of hearing a wonderful story from old Flip dissolved completely and he became silent as he was nearly all of his life, morning and noon and night.

He put his hand in the old man's as a kind of gesture of trust. Flip glanced over his shoulder at once to see if his master was watching from the stoep. No, the stoep was empty, nobody to notice; and in another minute they would be over the shale ridge and descending towards the Kamkam river. He gathered the boy's limp fingers in his rough palm and they went on, thinking their own thoughts.

The boy was not allowed to hold old Flip's hand nor to play with Flip's two grandchildren who were coloured a dark reddish brown and had hair like a dirty black woollen cap. He did not know why or question it but took it as something from which there was little escape like the long lack of rain that was ruining his father and mother. He did not know what it really was like to have a friend and he had to make one up.

His father gave him permission to go out with Outa Flip when the sheep were in the Kamkam river-bed so as to learn to recognise and count them. The outings were a grief to him now that the sheep were dying off so fast. Each time, he would come in and tell his father of the losses – so many more sheep never again to trail along the dusty tracks and drink at the wind-pump.

The boy's name was Crispus and his father was Nico Lubbe. They had come to the farm before he was born so that Crispus belonged to it by nature and was almost as much a part of the Karroo as Flip or the Grouberge mountains, blue across the skyline, or the Kamkam river. His father, Nico, did not belong there but was a stranger. He had been raised in a poor family in the Transvaal, leaving school before he got very far. He held jobs as a lorry driver and a garage-hand and a bottle-store assistant, always convinced the work was beneath him and that life was cheating him of his fair due. It was while he was selling liquor that he married Rina de Witt, and with that his luck seemed to change. She was pregnant with Crispus when they got the news, like a dazzling flash from the sky, that she had inherited from an uncle a farm in the Karroo. They sold their furniture, packed what they could into Nico's second-hand Hudson and set off. Behind for ever in the Transvaal was the life of debt and makeshift and social inferiority. They talked on the way of what their son might be – they were convinced it was a son. Nico had said exultantly, and yet with a touch of bitterness at his own lack of opportunity: 'With the land under his feet, the world will be open to him. Ja, he will go to university at Stellenbosch. What a choice for him! He could go into Parliament. He could be Prime Minister.' He knew it was fantastic but it satisfied his personal shortcoming to mention something so lofty and unattainable, almost holy, like the office of Prime Minister.

'No man, Nico,' Rina said. 'We should be content if he is an ordinary child and loves his parents.'

That was the moment of their highest bliss and success and good fortune. Arriving at the village of Roesdrif the colour of things began to change. Nobody had heard of the farm 'Liberty' which was their heritage. At last they settled matters through the lawyer Kalk in the larger town of Hamansdorp and took occupation of 'Liberty'. There they found the Kamkam river had never been known to run; no stock went with the land, no fences; the farmhouse was a two-roomed mud building with a thatch roof and reed ceiling. The only asset was Outa Flip who lived with his daughter Truitjie and her two baby children in a hut among a growth of prickly pears. He had a stringy little flock of goats, some donkeys and a contraption with two iron plough-wheels that he called a cart. The farm was already bonded, but lawyer Kalk gave Nico credit to put up a wind-pump and buy sheep. Crispus, the future Prime Minister, was born in Hamansdorp because Nico still had his Hudson then. He was a weak baby and took a long time learning to walk, but by the time he could get about confidently his heritage had disappeared. Lawyer Kalk handled the whole affair so astutely that Nico and Rina never discovered with any exactness who had dispossessed them. They no longer had title to a morgen of land, yet Nico clung obstinately to 'Liberty', paying a hire through Kalk that gave him half-formed suspicions about the value of the place. His animosity had turned into an almost insane violence of feeling aimed at the powers he thought he saw ranged in enmity against him – the banks, the Jews, the English, the Roman Catholic Church, even the Freemasons. They were his enemies; enemies of all like him, of the honest God-fearing people, of his entire nation. Even though they had robbed him of his birthright he would wait, he would not give up his footing on the land. Nico had put glass in his four small windows and a plank floor over the stamped clay of the two rooms. Since then, time had passed and it was six years ago the front door had last been painted; flakes of whitewash were peeling from the walls. He saw beyond this famished little spot on the Karroo veld to a day of wrath in which he would be set right and come into full possession of his earthly portion. From the time he had lost his Hudson he had been unable to take part in politics. It was too undignified, altogether too humiliating to arrive in the village in a donkey-cart or on foot for a political rally. So, bitterly, he had given it up and sneaked in unnoticed once in a few months, bought a newspaper and a bottle of brandy and

picked up the political talk. It had to suffice – that and speaking about his son Crispus. He would say as casually as his
trembling voice allowed how Crispus was turning out. 'You
can't believe it. That boy surprises me. Like an eagle he is,
so young but flying beyond his years.'

They were contemptuous of Nico Lubbe the interloper,
of his inexcusable poverty in the midst of their well-being.
They could see how he had struggled unsuccessfully to tidy
himself up, hack off the growth of beard and trim his hair.
He was a whiteman slipping backwards. Pitiful, the way his
lips shook as he spoke and the knob of his throat wobbled
up and down in a tremulous dance of anxiety. Nobody took
any notice of what he said, though some of them humoured
him and some made jokes at his expense.

Crushed by his visits, he would tramp home to 'Liberty',
stop to talk to himself and sometimes address imaginary
meetings – his audience a crow on a post or a bunch of panting sheep each with its head under another's belly for shade
against the scorching sun. Nico had made the 'law' to keep
Crispus from contamination by the coloureds. No playing,
no mixing whatever with Outa Flip, Truitjie or the two little
Hotnots. To them, the child was 'Basie' – the little Baas.
They touched their foreheads to him; as servants they recognised his destiny. Rina saw that the 'law' was kept too,
knowing from her own experience what was the fate of mixing. She had played as a child with black and coloured companions on the shabby side of a Free State village and
remembered with shame the day she first understood being
called a 'poor little white Kafir'. Neither Rina nor Nico could
see their son's slight limp. They loved watching his childish
movements and thought him cute with his grave little head
held a shade to one side.

Outa Flip and the boy stood a moment on the shale ridge before descending to the shallow basin of the Kamkam river. A scrubby line of white-thorn trees marked the course of the river, leafless the trees were, maybe quite dead. Sparse Karroo-bush grew close to the ground, whitened and sapless too. They could see sheep standing among the hot stones, heads drooped, twitching their tails at the flies. Flip and Crispus walked slowly to let the whole view sink in on them gradually. The boy's fingers wriggled as if for closer comfort in Flip's hand. Both were barefoot and their patched, faded clothes gave the old man little balance in the sheer witness of poverty. Crispus wore an old hat of his father's, shapeless, brimless, hanging down at the back to his shoulders. The old man had a sand-coloured cap he had made of meercat skins.

'You know, Outa Flip,' Crispus said, 'I had a dream the river was full of water.'

'Ag, now *that* was a dream.'

'Yes, and the water flowed up strong right to my father's stoep.'

'Well now!'

'What kind of things do you think would be in a beautiful river like that?'

'Dead donkeys,' Flip said.

'Ag, I mean live things.' The boy swung round to face Outa Flip and fixed on him his deep brown eyes glowing with animation. Flip's face was, taken bit by bit, so ugly it could scarcely be human. His bottom lip sagged thick and red, showing a straggling line of black teeth like rotten fence-posts; he had a small nose with huge nostrils that looked like the muzzle of Nico's double-barrelled shot-gun, and with his black eyes half hidden in creases and the sparse

28

hairs grey on his jowl there was not much to admire. Crispus did not admire Outa Flip; he loved him. Behind that rough face was a strange, warm content as changeless as the blue sky. There were his endless, cunning turns of cleverness and the fun of his stories told with a dozen different voices and mad antics that made you roll on the ground with laughter.

'There would be sea-cows in the river,' Crispus said earnestly.

'Sea-cows – yes, certain.'

'And what else do you think there were?'

'Ducks.'

'I don't mean common things. There were white birds as big as an ostrich – swans. And fish, so beautiful they were, they swam and frisked about, I could see them at the bottom of the river there among the sheep. Yes, one of the fishes was gold all over and it jumped up straight into the sky, shining. I woke then. There were other things and I'll remember them and tell you if I dream it again.'

'Ah, that was a nice dream – nice. And you were not afraid, seeing the river right up to the stoep?'

'Afraid? – But no.'

'Not just a little bit scared in your tummy?'

'Ag no, Outa Flip.'

'You don't know what fear is, my basie.'

They were walking on again and the boy thought seriously.

'I do,' he said a moment later. 'I had a fear my ma would die.'

'That's not being scared,' the old man answered. 'It's just knowing. You know some things that are sore, and other things that are gladsome. What I mean is this: being scared at night or out here in the wild, alone. Look now, you are not scared of your friend.' Flip looked sharply down at his little companion, smiling. The boy was greatly offended and and jerked away his hand. He pouted sullenly and there was a stronger shadow on his brow than that made by his tufty, bleached hair. They would have gone on, estranged, if the old man had not suddenly given a little husky shout of *'Daai 'sy!'* and ducked aside to rouse a large black and gold scorpion basking on a stone. The insect reared about to face the provocation of old Flip's whip handle. As it raised its poisoned sting he caught it cleverly and put it in his pocket.

'We'll find another one and have a fight,' he chuckled. 'My one should win – he's bigger than most, and so black, poisonous.'

He found another scorpion near the parched trees in the river-bed, and they squatted in the sand to watch the two venomous creatures fight.

'Never touch them,' old Flip said.

'Why do you do it?'

'No, I know just how. And besides – well, it makes no difference. If they sting me what does it matter?'

The scorpions were locked together with their pincers and searching the segments of one another's bodies with their stings for a vulnerable spot.

'Why do they fight?' Crispus said. 'They belong to the same kind.'

'Ag, they are stupid.'

'Look now, Outa Flip, your one's been stung.'

'If you listen well you will hear them scream.'

'Sies, horrid!' the boy stood up. 'I don't like seeing them, Outa Flip. Let's leave them and count the sheep.'

They walked home with the sun almost vertical above

and shadows a dark blotch at their feet. Crispus approached the house from the back. He knew his father would be sitting alone in the living-room, morose, staring at nothing through the open door while his mother cooked in the lean-to at the back. Quietly he slid into the stifling small kitchen and sat on a box. Rina brightened, seeing the one she loved to call her dear little ray of sunshine.

'What did you see, my treasure?'

Crispus took off his hat and ruffled his stiff hair. 'You will be glad, Ma.' He smiled gaily, giving her a moment of happy suspense. 'All the sheep are still alive.'

'God be thanked.'

'Outa Flip did not have to bring back any skins.'

'Father! All will come right.' She looked into the pot of boiling dry mealies.

'Ma, I have given up my friend.'

She turned to him with a grave smile. Her face was fat but the eyes sunken and dark-ringed and her skin grey and dull with exhaustion. 'Why, my little treasure, have you had a quarrel?'

This talk saddened her unutterably. Only when the child's loneliness tapped at her aching heart did she feel her resignation had reached its limit and her dreadful lot could no longer be borne. Crispus had had his 'friend' for quite a while. Sometimes he took his friend a scrap of food. He would play among the aloes and stunted karroo shrubs that grew on the koppie overlooking the house, and come back saying his friend was well. Sometimes his friend went away and they could not play. She humoured his tender and lively imagination.

'No, Ma,' he said, 'we have not quarrelled.'

But he would add nothing more. He did not care to admit

31

that Outa Flip was the cause of it. Flip had teased him about his friend, and because he loved old Flip he took it to heart more than he would otherwise have done. Rina could see how his mood changed and he became dejected. She took a rusk from a tin, spread some lard on it and gave it to him. If only she could satisfy his hopeless longings, if she could find him a real friend. His thoughts often amazed and perplexed her. It was true he was an eagle, as Nico said, but what strange flights he made, what a sorrowing world his lovely wings must carry him through.

He sat there moodily turning the tasty rusk about in his fingers and he began to nibble at it on one side and another. His eyes flickered to dart her a mischievous look. He had hidden a piece of rusk inside his patched blouse. Slipping off the box, he stood at the entrance to watch a hen scratching in the dusty yard. He edged out, holding his hat rolled up in one hand, and went off unhurriedly towards the higher ground that rose to the rocky crest of the koppie. Always in the past he had said he was taking a scrap he had saved for his friend. Today, he was secretive and had gone out without a word. Rina watched him go, his head a shade to one side. That he limped would not have occurred to her, and in any case the stony, uneven path concealed it. She saw him unroll his hat and put it on. He had now become full of purpose and his head and shoulders bobbed higher and higher up the slope of the koppie. Gradually she shifted across the doorway to keep him in sight. He took a turning to the left and in a minute was out of her view.

Rina reached down her sun-kappie from a nail and pulled it on, tying the tapes thoughtfully under her chin. She was going to see Crispus's shadow-play with his 'friend'. It would need care, for he must not know she was peeping.

Her ankles were puffy and swollen and the strap of her home-made sandals hurt as she stepped heavily up the path. Climbing higher, she could look over the thatch roof of her house, all reddish with dust. There also was Outa Flip's hut in its straggling ring of prickly pear on the far side of a dry donga. Truitjie, Flip's daughter, was walking up from the wind-pump with a paraffin tin of water on her head. One of her children, a sprightly little girl, trod methodically behind in her footprints. Rina had not yet come in sight of Crispus and was in no hurry. She did not wish to surprise him.

Now she no longer looked back but was all eyes for the first glimpse of her little boy. He was in a dun-coloured hat against the dun rocks and the parched bushes, terribly elusive. The sun glared and the heat brought the sweat out in a dew on her face. He was sure to see her first. After all, her kappie was white and he had sharp eyes, had Crispus. Perhaps she should go back and leave him to his game. She pushed aside the stiff flaps of the bonnet and wiped her face on her sleeve. My, what heat. And no longer a breath of wind.

Ag, she had come so far, why not carry on? Rina blew out a big breath and continued. She did not know the very slowness of her pace would bring her almost on top of Crispus without his seeing her. She was not quite expecting to catch up with him so soon. The path turned down and made a dip towards the donga behind Outa Flip's. Crispus must have left it about here and she also branched off, taking the slope of the koppie gradually. She plodded on one slow pace after another, dragging her long skirts past the wiry dry bushes. Then she stopped near a boulder and touched it. The stone was scorching hot, nearly hot enough, she thought, to fry

B

an egg. She looked over it, and there was Crispus on the other side, not six paces distant. He had his back to her and was bending down intent on something. A moment later he stood up with a little crow of a laugh, and she saw his 'friend'. Sliding down towards him out of a low crevice in the rocks she watched a huge yellow Cape cobra. Foot after foot of its loathsome body slipped out. Its neck touched the dust at the boy's feet and there began to form into a coil while the head rose, swaying up nearly to the height of his waist. Rina's hand was at her throat. She had first gulped and that gulp had helped her stifle back a shriek. What if she had screamed, she thought wildly; the snake would certainly have bitten her boy. So this was his friend, not imaginary at all as she had blindly believed. And every minute of his playtime with it he had been in deadly peril. So treacherous and vile a thing – one tiny slip and its poison fangs would be in her little treasure's cheek. She must fly home for Nico to blow the snake in pieces.

Rina moved fast, and fervently she prayed to God to spare her ray of sunshine. Surely, surely O Lord God, thy hand was with him all this time, Lord, merciful Redeemer, save him again until his father can destroy this thing of evil and horror. She was on the path, running.

'Nico! – Nico! – the gun, quick!' She began calling before she reached the house. He could not hear, but she drew breath in gasps, shouting: 'Quick! come, Nico, the gun!'

Rina burst into the living-room and her husband got up slowly from the bench, looking at her as if she had gone raving mad. It took her precious, wasted minutes before she could make him understand. Then he snatched the twelve-bore and loaded it with buck-shot, groaning aloud in his agony. In his mind he saw Crispus already dead, or writhing in the last throes of the cobra's venom.

'Nico,' she whispered again and again, 'do be so careful. They must not see you.'

'I understand,' he grunted.

He cocked both hammers of the gun so the click should not give him away when he was near. He was gripping Rina's hand and the two of them hurried to save their treasure, the only thing left to them in life. Nico had not had time to put on a hat; his grey hair was unkempt, weeks of salty bristles stood on his chin and lips and his dark eyes had wakened to a ferocious life.

'Here,' she said at the point to turn off the path. Nico went ahead now, drawing away steadily, but he glanced back and she signalled him which way to go. He found the boulder and carefully peered over with the care of a trained stalker. Crispus was sitting in the dust and the snake had its head raised level with him. He put out his hand and stroked its small dark head and neck. The snake flicked its skin hood half-way out and closed it as if it enjoyed being caressed. The boy was talking to it happily. Nico heard him say: 'It will never rain. Outa Flip says the storm-bird is bringing rain, but the rain clouds will not listen to it. He made two scorpions fight in the Kamkam. . . .'

Nico got the barrel up to the edge of the rock and he waited, feeling his heart turn under his ribs with an unaccustomed pain. All depended fatally on him. The cobra's head swayed out about an arm's length in front of Crispus and hovered there a moment. He was on the hair-breadth point of firing when it swayed back. He felt cold, thinking: If I had fired and missed! The boy held something in his hand and the cobra wove its head from side to side as he had seen snakes do to hypnotise their prey. And it swiftly scooped with its open jaws, taking the food.

'God Almighty!' Nico said to himself.

He could not get a sight on the snake and each moment he watched across the corner of the rock was like the slow passing of a year. He decided to draw his son's attention. First he whistled a bird-call softly; repeated it louder, and again yet not a true call so that Crispus would notice. The boy looked round but did not see him. So he whistled again, raising his head.

'Pa!' Crispus said, turning away his face.

'Come here, boy, but slowly, come to me.'

Crispus seemed to shiver, whether with fear or from weeping Nico could not see. He sat, keeping his head down, between Nico and the snake.

'Come to me, son,' Nico hissed louder. And at that moment the cobra saw him. Moving with deadly swiftness it rose up above Crispus and spread its hood. For a moment that was like all death and eternity he waited for it to strike the boy. And at the end of that wait he understood its awful move – it was protecting the child. It ducked suddenly as if in a feint and uncoiled quick as a whip, straight for Nico to attack him. A swing took it out of line with the boy and the instant it raised its head again to get him in sight, Nico fired.

Crispus scrambled to his feet dazed by the roar in his ears and the hot blast of gunpowder. First he saw nothing, and next, at his feet was the bloody, headless body of the cobra lashing about in huge mad convulsions. It was a tangle of gold coils, five feet in length, splashed with its own cold, red blood. He burst into a fit of crying.

Nico climbed over the rock and touched his son on the

36

shoulders. The lad was kneeling down trying with his hands to soothe and calm the writhing body of the snake. Only then did he look up at the man and the gun. His father had killed his friend. Crispus raised his clenched fists and rushed at Nico.

'Why did you shoot him?' he screamed. Nico leaned the gun against a stone, astonished, and tried to take up the boy in his arms. But Crispus wriggled free and fell in the dust, sobbing.

Rina found her husband on one knee patting the boy and muttering gruff things in a confused effort to console him. She stared, haggard, over the rock at the two of them and the snake coils quivering in the sun.

'He's all right,' Nico said.

They led Crispus down the koppie between them and he seemed to shrink away from his father and cling fast at Rina's side. She used her skirt to wipe the loathsome blood from his face and hands, though his blouse remained spattered and his hair was clotted and he looked ghastly. Outa Flip had heard the shot and came up at a shuffling run, followed by Truitjie and her girl and boy. Breathless, the coloured folk met the white people on the path and bunched up, every line of expression on their four faces a huge wondering question mark. But the white people were too distraught to say anything and with an unspoken understanding that words could wait they all started to walk on in a file.

None of them had gone more than a few steps when Crispus turned and said with a sob: 'Outa Flip – Pa has shot my friend.'

Then everybody began talking together.

'O, it's so sad,' said Truitjie.

'What's so sad then?' Rina burst out.

'The poor boy, my noointjie. He had to play with some-one.'

'But – a cobra!'

'Ja, that was his friend.'

'Then you knew. Oh my God!'

'Ja,' she said, and old Flip nodded guiltily, and the coloured children nodded also.

'They knew about him too,' Crispus said, looking at the children with passionate grief.

'All of you?' Nico demanded, his voice taking on an edge of fury.

'He wasn't dangerous, my baas,' old Flip said humbly. 'I took out the snake's teeth just to be, so to say, safe, my baas.'

Crispus was not listening. He was gazing at Flip's grand-children while no one else said anything. Nico and Rina were stunned and the coloured folk sensed in their hearts the great tautness like the gut string of a ramkie tuned almost to breaking. All of them, the two lonely familes, trudged on again to the house. It was the kind of occasion, like a birth or a death or a christening, when barriers fall down imperceptibly and there is a subtle feeling of get-together. Crispus eyed the children sideways as they went along. He turned to look up at his father's gun swinging on his shoulder against the sky which was hard and uncracked and was still without clouds.

In the docks where Roppie came to make his soft living one may see placarded in large clear lettering such notices as this: *'Lumkela isilenge ya usebenzazo!'* Which means – Watch out for cranes when working. It is written for the benefit of the Xhosa dockers in their own language, and they are men who work. Such a notice would be meaningless to Roppie; he is not a Xhosa, but perhaps more to the point, he is no worker, neither for himself nor for his family nor for anybody else.

Roppie lived by his wits, and he lived well. He had the kind of mental sharpness, a sense of superiority, that led him to despise honest labour and created a bias towards the product of other people's work. He was quite young, slim and venturesome, when first he arrived at the docks. The new era was a facile one in his life, a thriving and a flourishing that could be measured in stages by visible increases in weight. He looked sleek and black, his beard and whiskers were well groomed, and the tiers of double chins and the added inches of girth around his middle showed there was more cunning than exertion in the way he came by his daily meals. His gruff, good-natured voice was familiar to the wharf-men and tug-masters, crane-drivers and dockers.

He was missed the first time he disappeared, but it was not long before he was back – with a wife. The baby was scarcely a month old when he vanished again, no one knew where, and returned with a second wife. Not being a Xhosa, there were no difficulties about finding lobola, and with his un-Christian character he was able to live down the slur of bigamy. Unconcerned, he went on to find himself in succession a third and a fourth wife, and settled down to the natural order of procreation, and what can best be described as *die lekker lewe*; sweet content.

His favourite haunt was the middle of the Alfred Dock. There he could be seen on any bright day lolling voluptuously in the greasy water, turning up his blubbery paunch to the hot rays of the sun and generally luxuriating in such a display of pleasurable sensuousness as to be quite sickening. He would wave to you as you looked down from the quay and perhaps open his mouth lazily to belch or yawn contemptuously.

When the trawlers came in from the deep sea loaded down to the gunwales with stock-fish, not to mention soles, silver, gurnet, kingklip, cob, white and red stumpnose, skate, yellowtail and tunny, Roppie was there in the fish-harbour to meet them. He put on a display of aquabatics and sheer mirth-provoking clowning that infallibly won him a meal. His turns were inspired, and no mere circus seal with his rubber balls and tin trumpets and splashings in a muddy tank had any approach to the poetic frenzy of Roppie's act. Sometimes he put up a sham battle with a shark or an octopus that he found dead, foul-hooked or poisoned somewhere in the harbour, and his heroics were sure to draw a crowd of gullible admirers.

The fish thrown to him for his performance served two purposes. Anything fresh enough he swallowed at a gulp and the rest floated about as a kind of ground-bait to attract scavenging shoals. Roppie's family would surround the shoal-fish and drive them into a corner, into the dry-dock or against a shelving of the wharves, and there he went in and guzzled until the prey he tried to swallow slipped back through his teeth from pressure and lack of space. Then he wallowed off and left the others to take what they could. Gormandising, basking, dreaming of more debauches, that was the life of Roppie, the slippery downward path to decadence and ruin; greed begetting more greed, an appetite never denied, and all with an effortless ease that put layers of fat round the heart and bowels, hardened arteries and needled up blood pressure. His life was by all the usual standards a success. It would have continued a success had he not carried it too far.

On a pleasant summer morning with no wind and a sharp sting in the sun's rays, the old coaster *Mary-Ann* was towed up for alterations and a general overhaul in the dry-dock. There was the normal bustle of work in the Alfred Basin. Lines of doubly black Xhosa stevedores were bunkering the deep-sea trawlers *Cape Matapan* and *Blomvlei*, tipping their coal-baskets to a gay work chant. A diesel crusher was turning a truck-load of ice into a glittering avalanche of snow cascading down into the freezing-hold of the *Blomvlei*. The *Mary-Ann* was already fast in the open dry-dock, and two tugs smartly edged the tubby floating caisson into position across the dock mouth. In a few minutes the wharf-men would have the sea-cocks open and sink the caisson in its water-tight grooves. And after that traffic would roll over its bridge-head while the *Mary-Ann*, lying dry on its chocks, was hammered and scraped and riveted for a month or more.

All this busy flurry was above the surface in the sun's bland rays. The tugs with green and mustard-coloured funnels snorting and whooping as they signalled their moves, a clamour of riveters in the boat-yard, locomotives shunting a line of petrol tank-cars and sea-gulls in a shrill whorl over the closing dock.

The gulls knew from long habit that a dry-docking was a gala event for them. Always some pickings appeared when the pumps drained the lock, at times a foot deep of struggling, flashing silver, a gargantuan repast, a riot of gorging and regurgitation and gorging again for the sheer lust of bird-brained gluttony. That morning they were in for a surfeit.

Below the surface there was already going on an orgy of rapacity. The seals had driven in a shoal of haarders and maasbankers, and Roppie was in the thick, opening his wide maw and sliding forward to cram himself to the ears with live, wriggling delicacies. He closed his teeth, blew out the water and lunged for more. There were millions of them, a meal for a pod of whales, and Roppie could have only one regret – that the law of Nature gave him a belly of such limits. He knew the moment to slip out before the caisson settled into its grooves, and the other seals knew too. They had never been caught, and somewhere in their instinct for survival was the awareness that to be trapped there was death. For a month or two the lock remained closed, and nothing that went in alive ever came out. Only the ships floated out with the new red paint on their bottoms and bronze screws shining.

The smaller members of the family, the wives and young-lings, had already taken fright and swum past the slowly sinking caisson into the open basin. But Roppie made another turn among the jammed and struggling shoal, the water almost solid at the far end with fish. If he could get no more inside his stomach he could enjoy the sensation of rubbing his flanks against them, rolling in provender. He surfaced near the stern of the coaster and belched up some pilchards and a haarder. A wharfie shouted and waved angrily at him, and he waved back a languid flipper, lolled over in the water and dived again. Once more through the trapped shoal and then leisurely he swam for the entrance. There was no opening.

He swam up and down looking for the way out which had been wide and easy when last he cruised that way. But now there was no way out, the others had gone and the lock was closed; not a crack remained wide enough to pass a tadpole.

Roppie hurried to the upper end to look for an opening there. He was frightened and alert and paid no heed to the struggling mass of small fish that surged before him. Of course there was no way out that end. He swam up and down at the base of the dock walls, and at one spot sensed the outward rush of water. Here he thought was his loophole. But there was a grille of close iron bars over the channel. It was the outlet of the pumping circuit, and the pumps were going at full bore, draining the dock. Roppie circled the whole place again in a panic. His fear kept him from surfacing, and while he groped for an opening the sight of a diver working under the vessel struck a new terror into him. He was caught, doomed.

The water-level slowly sank and more and more of the dark, rusty hull of the *Mary-Ann* thrust up into the air. For a while Roppie lay still under the ship. He was exhausted and saving his strength. At last he poked his nose up carefully near the exposed rudder and took a breath. He was not seen. He moved to the upper end and hid among the fish. They took no more notice of him than of a weed-covered rock. They were doomed too.

The sea-gulls were screaming and plunging among the exposed fish. They flew off with the flapping silver prey in their beaks and perched on roof-tops and on the mast-heads of moored boats to cram down the fish with a few avid gulps. Cormorants dived into the mêlée. A lovely broad-winged malmock flew up with a big fish, dropped it and caught it again in mid-air as if to prove himself no mere scavenger. All the while Roppie lay quiet, and when at last the water had drained away and he felt the full weight of himself on the concrete, he raised his head among the fish and the whirring birds' wings, the cries of greed and triumph and anger.

The sky was a shape far above, bounded by lofty walls. It was the domain of the birds, and Roppie had nothing in common with them but their greed. He turned and began to move off, slithering among the layers of dying and faintly shuddering fish. Now he began to hear the shouts of humans. They were watching his fat, dark form ploughing its way along the length of the dock. Some were scaling down the iron ladders. He slid and lurched this way and that and his eyes bulged and he panted with terror. Wherever he looked now he saw humans. They were scooping up loads of fish in baskets and gunny sacks and buckets and sending them aloft by ropes to others leaning out across the sky-line. The birds darted recklessly between them and shrieked with derision if they could get away with a fish out of the very baskets. Roppie alone could not get away. He was heavy with over-eating and sick with fear. In several different ways he was slipping.

The humans did not try to harm him, but some of them were discussing what was to be done. There was no question of the contractors flooding the dock and opening the barrier to release him. The *Mary-Ann* would be under repair for at least six weeks, and forty days in the sun-broiled pit of the dry-dock was slow death for the sea dweller. The small chance of keeping him alive did not justify the cost of fresh food.

Messages were sent out and more humans arrived at the lip of the dock, dark figures with white caps, railway police, one of them armed with a rifle. He had come to give the prisoner the mercy shot.

All the while Roppie was lurching up and down with his clumsy dry-land gait, flippers and tail, flippers and tail. He looked quite small and pitiful down in the dock nearly fifty feet below. But from near-by, at his own level, he was truly bulky, and there was a fine sheen on his dark coat; his eyes were large and steady and sad, looking about uncertainly and then up at the impossibly distant blue sky.

It took longer than usual to clean out the dock bottom, scour away the mud and refuse and the unwanted dead fish and hose it all down. For a while Roppie lay in the shade of the *Mary-Ann*, looking out sadly and anxiously and breathing in long soft gasps. The policeman with a rifle had climbed down the stone steps at the inner end and was sitting on a wooden chock with the weapon against his knee. He did not like the task he had been given, and he did not look at the victim. The wall of the dock rose before him first in a tier of broad granite ledges several feet high against which the timber balks were wedged to support docked vessels. Higher up, the terraces were wider spaced, rising five or six feet at a time with a ledge of two or three feet. From below, the wall looked like a giant stairway advancing by ever higher steps to its granite lip.

A movement drew the policeman's attention. It was

Roppie slouching out into the direct sunlight. He had rested, he had taken stock in his instinctive way of the danger and with one glance up at the sky he began his supreme effort. A slow, sinuous heave raised his flippers and chest on to the first step and he drew his body up. At first a few men called to each other; heads appeared over the upper rim, men inside the dock stopped to watch and the policeman stepped out from the shade.

The first step had been easy. There was little room to shift about but the instinct of countless wild generations of rock climbers had not been dimmed even by years of soft living and he kept his balance as he heaved his great fat body up ledge after ledge, higher against the face of the dock wall. Now he was nearly half-way up, the height of a two-storey house, and he had reached the first of the steeper ledges. He could no longer count on slithering up as he had started. The next ledge was too high. If he were to get up now he had to to jump. Nearly five feet of vertical granite wall from one narrow ridge to the next, and below him, if he slipped, a fall to certain death.

Hundreds were watching him now. Fishermen left off repairing their nets and walked over to see what was going on. Warehousemen came with pencil stubs stuck over one ear and a shunter gripped his rolled-up flags and said: '*Allemagtig*! but he will never do it.'

Roppie gathered up his long soft body and with the queer sea-changed hind feet, webbed into a tough tail-fluke, he felt carefully for a grip on the stones. Suddenly, with a heave of head and chest and a mighty whip of the back he took the jump. The massive black body rose at first slowly from all its inertia like a rocket taking off and then straightened vertically. The flippers found a hold over the ledge and with a great shudder the whole length of him followed.

All the watchers held their breath a moment, then a sound like a sigh went up from them. The next jump was higher and Roppie was straining up his head to gauge it like a cat measuring her leap. Again he seemed to coil up every last ounce of his strength, taking a little longer and sending ripples as if of anxiety down his exposed side. The ledge was so narrow that a part of his bulk overhung it. He did not look down. Had he done so he would have seen the upturned faces of watchers, standing off at a distance in case he fell, and the receding tiers of ledges and a smooth, cruel floor down under him. He made the jump, precariously, and there was a shivering instant before he got his tail over and could adjust his balance. Three more jumps remained, each higher than the last, before he reached the summit. 'He'll never do it,' they said. 'He'll never do it.'

He took the next jump and lay for a longer time to rest. His weight and the heavy meal in his belly were telling against him. Then he raised his head and peered to measure the ledge above. He was a long way up now. The sky was nearer. He could see the edge of the masonry but he could not see that lying loose on the stone was a heavy iron ring, a rail-truck coupling that had fallen and rested there long enough to make a red rust-streak. The watchers above could see it, twelve feet or so below them, lying loose.

Roppie began coiling up for the jump. 'Get that link out of the way!' Somebody ran for a rod or plank to move the coupling. 'Don't frighten him!' They hadn't found anything long enough to reach, and he was on the point of making his leap. Once again that stupendous whip of the powerful back, the heavy head and chest rising vertically, and his flippers

47

were over the edge. But the main grip came down on the iron ring and it slipped. It slid outwards while the other flipper scrabbled wildly to take hold. Then his whole balance was lost and he fell.

He fell soft and yielding on the ledge from which he had jumped and his bulk rolled outwards. Perilously it hung poised on the rim and through him ran a strange rippling cat-like movement, the writhe of a cat's body by which it restores balance in mid-air. The movement saved him, flinging his weight against the wall, and he lay there with one flipper raised awkwardly in the air and a small trickle of blood running from his nose. For quite a long time he lay like that only faintly moving the flipper. The onlookers began talking, softly at first, hushed by a feeling of awe and pity and admiration for the injured creature.

Then by degrees Roppie edged himself round until he had his weight fairly poised and he rested his head on the stone. The sun was blazing full on him and a little circle of blood gathered near his nose.

They did not know what to do. The policeman with a rifle had climbed out again and was looking down. Voices urged him to put the wild thing out of its suffering. Others said: 'Give him time, give him a chance.' He did not know what to do.

Roppie looked up and took his time measuring the height to the ledge. 'He's going to try again,' they said. He had the instinct not to try in the same place and very carefully he heaved himself forward about three lengths. There he gathered himself quite slowly, quivering like a lion arching its haunches for the charge. And he jumped. He got over this time and there was a great cheer as if a winning try had been scored in the rugby final. The sea-birds wheeled against the blue and the Xhosa coal-heavers in a black bunch laughed loudly but tensely.

The last leap to the summit was the highest and there was not a man in that wide amphitheatre whose heart was not with the climber. The policeman with the rifle cleared a space so he would not be hindered; after the cheer a hush had come and everyone waited. The boom of the midday cannon sent a start through them.

Roppie took a long and calculated time over that last tremendous leap, and he made it. He was out in the open, on the flat, hot paving and he raised himself on his flippers to look round while the cheering surged up and faded. Quite deliberately and unafraid of the humans, he lurched over the roadway and rail-track and he paused on the brink of the quay. Fifteen feet below him the greasy green water sucked at the stones and threw up reflections from the high sun. Out in the middle of the basin some of his family were basking unconcerned. Beyond them was the ship channel leading to the fish harbour and the Victoria Dock, and beyond the breakwater again the open sea. The blood was crusted on his nose and whiskers and his sides heaved.

With a flip of his tail-flukes he dived and disappeared. He bobbed up once near the entrance to the ship channel, swimming strongly and not pausing to look at his wives. He passed the docks and the breakwater. He was making for the wild fishing-grounds of the deep Atlantic. And he never came back.

The train seemed to be slowing down. The wheels shrieked on the metals and the roar and grind came up through the floor with a continual vibration. Cold air blew in gusts through the half-opened window which had been jammed and could not be closed up or lowered. The frosted-glass pane glinted in the light from a single small electric bulb and through the open part she could see the black night sprinkled with faint stars which seemed to sway above the veld with the movement of the train. She gazed out, yearning for the peace the stars had so often distilled over her, and tears swelled and rolled down her face.

The officials had stopped banging on the door. They had stopped shouting. But she knew they were there. A foot scuffled in the dusty corridor outside and her heart bounded in terror. She was sitting on the floor, weak and light-headed. Somehow she had managed to tidy herself up and even to clean the floor and now she waited, not knowing what might come, not knowing the consequences of her crime. Looking into the black square of the night, she thought again of her husband, Motsibo Lefela, so far away across the world that she might never see him, and she rocked her head in hopelessness.

Those officials came back to the door and this time they had something heavy. At the first crash she dragged herself to her feet and squeezed into one corner. She had wrapped her new-born baby in her petticoats and made a big soft bundle of him with her pink and grey striped blanket. Down in its folds she could see part of the tiny dark face and the blue-black eyes gazing up, unseeing, into the light. They were coming for him – for her and for him. All the strength was in their hands. Behind their cold pale eyes was something past understanding – some law they would use against her, some reason no one would ever see but themselves.

Crash! Crash! The door bolts held. The train was running against its brakes down long curves into a valley. For a flash the lights caught against rock sides of a cutting and then emptiness, the black night and the swinging stars. She lurched across to the window and lifted up the soft bundle. She had not named him. 'Baby, baby, baby . . .' she cried to herself. She pushed him quickly through the open gap into the night, and he fell and was gone. She had nothing left. No desire to go on living, no gladness, no terror or pain.

They broke down the door of the third-class toilet and found the native woman passenger facing them, with a blank look and her mouth open as if she were dead on her feet. The ticket examiner stood in the door frame, a heavy man with small blue eyes in a broad red face and braid on his peak cap. The veins of his neck and temples were almost bursting with fury. A railway policeman in dark blue with silver buttons peered over his shoulder and behind him were more faces, white and brown and black. They saw the bloodstains on the woman's dress and in the basin and the examiner started bawling at her. He stopped in the middle of a word. She had suddenly crumpled and, looking at her in a heap on the floor, he turned paler.

'My Lord – she's passed out!'

Slowly the train pulled out into the night. The little

station on the veld was quiet and its few lights shone against the encircling darkness. The young woman sat on a plank bench in the third-class waiting-room which was an open shack near the line. A coat had been put round her shoulders, a man's coat. The man – it must be his – was tending a fire on the earth floor. Intermittently the wind nagged at the shack, rattling the iron. It swirled up smoke from the fire which could do nothing to take the edge off the cold. The woman's body and legs were numbed and she could not feel her feet at all. Inside her was an enormous space of aching. Two policemen, one white and one black, stood in long blue greatcoats at the doorless entrance to the shack, stamped their feet, yawned and blew out little puffs of smoke from their pipes.

The man at the fire stood up at last and brought her a tin can of hot coffee. Sitting on the bench at her side, he first took a sip and then held the can to her lips.

'*Ausei* (sister), drink this. It will help you.'

She turned her head away. Then she took the can in both hands and drank greedily, spilling drops down her chin. She glanced at him and he answered the unspoken question in her eyes.

'I have told them I am your cousin. My name is Paul Moleng.'

'Why am I here, father?'

'Why is anyone here?' he answered and his teeth showed in a cheerful but patient smile like a man teaching his child. 'Sleep now. In the daylight there will be time to talk.'

She sat staring and something came back to her. 'He said I had murdered my baby. . . . He said I murdered my baby. . . .' She repeated it over and over as if the words had no meaning. 'Why did he say that? Tell the policeman my baby is safe. I tied him up myself – he is a boy – and I will feed him when he cries.'

'I will tell him, my sister.'

Paul Moleng lifted her feet up and laid her on the bench. He took a blanket from his case and covered her with it. Yes, he too wondered how she had come to be there. The passenger list recorded her name as Eva Lefela and the police were holding her for child-murder. He had got off the train at the station to help her. Others had also wanted to stay and help, but he had said: 'I know something of the law and I can watch over her. Not all of us can be her brother.'

They took up a collection and he had four pounds and some shillings in his pocket for her when he climbed down on the cinders of the lonely platform a thousand miles from his destination. The train had left and now they were waiting for a police squad car to come up from the district centre. There was nothing much he could do for the girl beyond seeing she got her legal rights.

She lay motionless and at long intervals a moan forced its way past her lips. It would soon be dawn. The up express train came thundering through the station without slowing down; its corridor lights flickered in confusing patterns inside the shack, and then its din faded into the distance. The wind died and the night fell so quiet they could hear the call and answering cries of jackals across the veld. Geese in some unseen farmyard raised a faint cackle. A sheep bleated. . . . The African police guard moved in nearer the fire and squatted beside Moleng.

'The frost will be thick in the morning,' he said.

'E, thick and white.'

They did not say anything more. Outside, the white policeman's boots plodded in the cinders, step after slow step, as he walked up and down to kill time. Paul Moleng fixed his eyes on the coals and tried to keep his thoughts from the little brown body that must be lying somewhere alongside the rail-track.

The girl was awake. She turned her face to the two men at the fire, sighed and turned back. The frost would be thick and white in the morning. Would she ever see the morning? She no longer had any longing to live. Never again could she face Motsibo, her husband. When she had left home – her home and his – the frost had sparkled on the grass and there was snow shimmering on the peaks of the Thaba Putsua mountains. The sun had risen above the snow turning it pale pink like apple blossom and the small clouds were a deeper colour. Often she had seen the sun rise but never in such peace and softness. She had taken it as a sign and said to her husband's brother riding at her side: 'Look – it is God who blesses this day.'

Isaiah Lefela, who had only one leg, for the other had been crushed in a mining accident, looked into the sunrise and the light was like gold on his skin. 'E,' he answered in a mild tone, 'every day is as good as we take it.'

He of all the village people had not opposed or thwarted her, and she felt he was like a brother and a father and guardian to her during the long months she waited for Motsibo to come home. Motsibo worked in Cape Town in a cement factory and sent home to her in Basutoland what he saved from his wages. In her sixth month she had a vivid dream that her baby had been born and could not breathe. It choked and its face swelled up to a ghastly size. But Motsibo came and took it, and as soon as he gave it a name it started to breathe. Then it smiled and clapped its hands together.

She had not told anyone her dream because she was a Christian with a school education and knew such a dream would arouse strong feelings among the older people – fears that ran deep in their hearts. But she had written to Motsibo to make sure he came home for the birth. The thought of having her firstborn without her husband near-by now filled her with more than anxiety – with a cold black dread. He had written promising to be home well on time. In two months his service contract ended and three days after he was paid off he would be home in his own hilly district above the Mekhaling river.

Then a terrible blow had fallen. The Government issued a new control regulation to check native workmen from re-entering a city. Motsibo found that once he left Cape Town to see his wife he might never be allowed to return to that or any other town to seek employment. Nothing would remain but to work for the white farmers at a shilling a day – fifteen pounds a year. From that he could not feed himself and pay his taxes nor support his family. He must stay in Cape Town until some way could be found out of this iron trap.

Eva had walked three miles down winding paths to the store and found his letter waiting, and as she read it the blue notepaper with Motsibo's sharp handwriting shook in her fingers. Her friends thought she had been taken ill. A horse was found to carry her home and her mother-in-law tied a medicine-charm round her stomach.

She told them a few days later that she was going to Cape Town to be near her husband for the birth of the baby. Nothing could bend her from the decision, no threats or warnings or prophecies could shake her will. In all this the one who stood by her was the smiling, courageous Isaiah.

He would come hopping along to the rondavel with the help of his home-made wooden stump to talk and joke with her.

'Let her go – in her heart she knows best,' he told the others.

'You are a one to talk!' his mother reproached him with his bodily defect. But when Isaiah was in the saddle of his pony with his tall straw hat on and a blue and yellow blanket across his shoulders he was as proud and gay as any man, and no one could think of him as a cripple.

Eva's homeland knew what poverty was. Poverty and stagnation drove out the young men like Motsibo to work. And when they left the hazy fastness of Basutoland they stepped into a foreign world, the world of South Africa that ringed them on all sides. She thought Paradise was a mountainous land where the angels rode calmly on sleek horses and their talk was like a song and the noise their bit chains made was like guitar music. God sat on a cloud-reaching summit like Thaba Putsua, continually showering down blessings, peace and glory on all while listening to the swell of their psalms. She did not think of the English in Paradise. The English ran the government and police, the offices, the labour recruiting posts and most of the stores. There were English missionaries too, as well as French, Americans and Germans, though her own pastor was a grey-haired Mosuto. English Government was mild and polite, even helpful. Mostly it left people alone or gave them half-hearted advice. It was like the love of a stepfather.

She had never been over the border into South Africa, and so everything she knew about it reached her from others. Many wild and improbable things came into the picture she had – yet there was no mistaking the expression on men's faces and the vibration in their words when they spoke of it, men who knew from experience such as Isaiah, who came back maimed. Although he did not complain and was not a bitter man, she thought she could read things in his heart. South Africa, to her, was the land of the *maburu* (Boers). However many others lived there, it was still so. All her feelings towards that outer circle were rolled up into a deep and whispering fear. And she knew now that she had to go there, unaided, against the wisdom of her people, for the one overwhelming reason that she must have Motsibo at her side when their baby came.

She thought she had a month to go when she drew some of her money from the Post Office savings bank and tied it in a knot in a square of red cotton. Isaiah lent her his suitcase for the journey, the one he had brought on his last homecoming. She packed a few garments, a towel and the baby clothes she had made and collected over the long summer and autumn months.

They had got up before dawn, and by the time they were ready there was a crowd gathered among the rondavels of the village wrapped up to the eyes in warm blankets. Sleepy children clung to their elders' legs, men murmured together in groups smoking slender-bowled pipes. Not one of them, except Isaiah, approved of her going, but now that they saw her strained face and the tears always below the surface of her eyes, they kept back any harsh words. They brought small gifts of food for the journey in the train and Motsibo's mother gave her a *lebanta* belt to take to him with a medicine charm for luck and health. One of the young women approached Eva shyly and gave her £1 3s. 6d. all in shillings and sixpences. The money had been collected among them and with each coin she placed in Eva's palm she said in a soft voice: 'This is from Khopiso, this is from Masebo, this is from me, this is from Mamosebetsi, the daughter of Letsieo. . .' As she continued the long list, Eva's head bowed and tears splashed into her hand among the silver coins.

Isaiah's piebald pony was standing ready saddled, and beside it a sturdy little grey. Some young men had come to see them off, and one said with a serious face: 'Ao, let her take Seeso's horse; it is strong and quiet. She is racing with some extra weight.'

Seeso led his horse forward readily. 'Ride him, he never loses, *ausei*.'

'Then tell me what prize I will win,' Eva replied.

They all laughed, turning to glance into one another's eyes. The strain of her departure seemed to have eased. She could not refuse the offer of the strong bay, and they shortened the stirrups and helped her up into the saddle. Isaiah rode ahead with the suitcase on his saddle-bow; Eva was next, and after her the young men followed to see her part of the way to Mafeteng. She looked back from the defile of the valley below the village and saw her people still standing there. Away beyond them rose the line of the mountains behind which the sun pushed long rays turning the clouds peach-coloured and touching the snow. The young men began a sad but beautiful song:

'*Matsidiso ngoana Rakhali,*
    Ha esale o tsamaea oa risiea
    Le bodudu oare o ea Gauteng. . . .'

('O Matsidiso the child of Rakhali,
    Since you must go, sadly we shall miss you

Saying you must journey there to the Gold-Mines. . . .')

Surely, she thought, this song comes from their hearts and is heard in heaven. It told a story so familiar to all of them. Isaiah was singing in harmony and birds flew up with a trill at their approach.

They reached Mafeteng in the warmth of the day. The post-bus was waiting in the crowded single street, although it was not due to leave for an hour. Seeing it there struck a blow at Eva's heart. It was the last link; it would rush her over the border into the land of the *maburu*. She closed her eyes for a few moments.

'I do not want to go.'

'Do you mean that, *ausei*?' Isaiah asked, looking closely at her. She thought he sounded relieved.

'No, I must go.'

He went to buy her a ticket and came back with one for himself as well. 'I will come with you to Wepener and put you on the train,' he said. 'Then surely someone will look after you until you see Motsibo.' There was so great a flood of gratitude in her look that he said nothing more. He did not mean to alarm her over the difficulties of buying a rail ticket, the questions that might be bawled at her in Afrikaans, which she barely understood, the delays and trials of a novice traveller.

It was only sixteen miles by road to Wepener, but the road led out of Basutoland into South Africa. To her imagination it was like a crossing into the terrifying un-known, and she clung with a feeling of desperation to Isaiah's side. They took their seats in the bus half an hour before it was due to leave, and, as the hard benches filled, her heart seemed to press into her throat, almost choking her. She did not hear what Isaiah said and could not have spoken a word. At last the motor started, there were calls and shouts and laughter from scores of people saying good-bye. Passengers leaned over the sides; one was crying, another was eating an orange. Mafeteng disappeared behind them in a billow of dust.

She expected something startling to happen, some strange experience always to be remembered when she crossed the border. At that point she would be, like her husband, wholly in the hands of those others. They would take her into their power. Such a sinister event needed all of a person's courage. She waited tensely while the people chatted and exchanged anecdotes. They all knew after the bus had travelled only a few miles that she was pregnant and was on her way to join her husband.

'Surely this is a strange thing,' one said.

'The husband should come to her.'

'Ao! Have you heard – there is the new law!'

'Who can keep count of the new laws? They make my brain dizzy.'

'No, brother, you must always be watchful down there.' He nodded towards the rolling country descending to the Caledon River beyond the border. 'Before you take a step, look behind you and in front, to the left and right, east, south, north, west, over your head and under your feet.'

'And still you get caught!'

There was a murmur of quiet laughter.

'E, what people – the *maburu*!'

'What people . . .'

'Here we are . . .'

The bus bounced over the culvert of a small gully. On one side was a board with the words 'UNION OF SOUTH AFRICA';

on the other side another board said: 'BASUTOLAND – BRITISH
TERRITORY'. They did not pause; the world was the same.
The sun still shone in a cloudless sky, and there they were,
a bus-load of people climbing the dusty, winding road to
Wepener. Eva tried to make herself believe she had crossed
the border, and the very ease of it made her shudder. Was
dying, too, as simple as this?

They had plenty of time. The daily passenger train left
that evening at 9.45. Eva went into the station with Isaiah.
She felt tired in her joints and a tremor fluttered through
her as she entered the building. Isaiah knew his way about
and he was tactful. He waited until the booking clerk was
unoccupied and approached him with Eva. He spoke careful Afrikaans, laid out all the correct papers and the fare
money. The *morena* would understand that this was an in-
experienced woman who needed a little help, he said, indeed
all the help she could get.

The *morena* was a young man with a pleasant sunburnt
face and blue eyes. He made out the ticket without a word
and then he came from his small office and chatted to Isaiah.
'Ah, I see,' he said with his eyes twinkling, 'she will soon be
needing two tickets.'

'One and a half, *morena*,' Isaiah said.

He was agreeably surprised that the official should be
affable, but he showed nothing in his broad, calm face. He
wanted to take advantage of this good beginning, to set at
rest some of Eva's anxiety. The *maburu* were one thing, but
each of them taken separately was a person who could be
courteous and even friendly. They talked a few minutes
about the making of roads and dams in Basutoland.

'*Sala hantle morena*,' he said in farewell, and the clerk
nodded. His eyes followed the one-legged man as he hobbled

off on his wooden stump, and he was thinking – that's a polite Kafir, he hasn't been spoilt.

Eva had grasped the meaning of the clerk's remark that she would soon be needing two tickets, and it put her into a great alarm.

'That was only the white man's idea of a joke,' Isaiah said.

'Ao!'

'He was smiling, *ausei*.'

'E, he was smiling.'

She watched the sun set in wild flares of changing colour. It was setting over South Africa, and it seemed to her even the great sun, like her, was falling a prisoner into strange hands. But to Isaiah she said nothing; he had had enough of her fears. He arranged with a passenger to give her help in changing on to the through mail train at Bloemfontein, and at last the time came when he watched her face recede and disappear in the darkness beyond the station platform.

In the compartment Eva sat jammed between other passengers on the hard wooden bench. The train's movement came as a relief to her; she leaned her head back, closed her eyes and let her body rock with the sway and spring of the coach. Some of the passengers slept, others talked in low voices. They would reach Bloemfontein about midnight.

Eva fell asleep.

The train was still flying with its deep incessant rumble over the veld when she woke. What it was that aroused her she did not know, except a vague stirring of unrest through her body. The light was on and all the people were asleep, heads and bodies swaying in a strange unison. She sat for a long time staring at nothing until it came again, a tingling, unmistakable contracting pain. No, no, no, she told herself, this is only a stomach-ache. No, it is the food I have eaten. She took two aspirins from a small bottle Isaiah had given her, chewed and swallowed them. Nothing happened until they were beginning to run past lights in the outer suburbs of Bloemfontein, when she had another but milder contraction. She took one aspirin. Yes, it was the food and unaccustomed travelling that had upset her.

Changing trains even at that hour, the unimaginably vast central station rang with sounds and was busy with hurrying people. More white people were there than she had ever seen together, all in smart winter coats. She felt stiff and ached, but the others carried her case and saw her into a place up in front of the through mail. The compartment was less crowded. They were not all Basuto, and among them were people of unfamiliar nations. She felt more estranged and remote.

The train pulled out with a long shriek of the whistle. Cold draughts crept through the compartment and the travellers seemed to huddle together with a sigh of resignation against the long, comfortless journey ahead. Eva sat tense, trying not to think of the thing she now most feared. Her hopes rose slowly and, slackening all her body into a pleasant drowsy feeling, she settled back to sleep. The pain suddenly welled up within and swept over her senses. Involuntarily she gave a cry. People looked at her in amazement.

'I had a dream,' she gasped.

They murmured commonplaces to comfort her while she closed her eyes and pretended to sleep. But it was no use. Panic was taking hold of her with each surge of the pain. Desperately she heaved herself up and made for the door over people's outstretched feet. A woman told her where to go as she pushed out into the cold corridor. She looked one way and saw a big white man in a dark uniform – the examiner making his round. She turned and staggered away from him, clinging to the brass hand-rail for support.

Once inside the small room, alone, she felt a new courage creep back into her heart. She had to face this time, and she did not have to be told what to do. Carefully she locked and bolted the door. The rest of the enormous world, the passengers, the train, the white officials; speed, journey and time faded out of her mind. She took off her three cotton petticoats and squatted down on her knees with her hands flat on the floor behind her. Sometimes her eyes were fixed on the electric bulb in the roof or on the black square of the half-open window, but she saw neither the light nor the stars. Sometimes her head fell forward and lolled on her breast. She did not utter a cry.

The little boy was born on her knees; her eyes cleared and she wiped his face. She put her finger in the tiny pink and brown hand and the fist closed sturdily on her. The face, already dear to her, wrinkled up for a cry.

'*Ngoana, ngoana, ngoana*'–'Baby, baby, baby,' she crooned over him.

She wrapped him in her petticoats, then in the thick folds of her grey and pink blanket, and was fastening the last corner with a big safety-pin when the door was tried. A heavy rap followed on the panels:

'Who's in here?' a voice shouted in Afrikaans.

It all came back to her in an oppressive deluge. She had done some terrible wrong. She remembered what the clerk had said – that she would need two tickets. Her dream returned to her, and the dread that she would lose her baby because Motsibo was not near to save him. They would

64

take her baby away: that was her punishment. In the little square room she was alone, and outside were the officials, the merciless power of the *maburu*. Bang– bang – bang on the door.

'*Maak oop!*' a fierce voice shouted again and again. 'It's no use hiding in there if you haven't got a ticket!'

She waited, crouching on the floor and breathing hard like a cat with its ears flat. There was silence for what seemed a long time, and then the scuffling of feet again; more of them, more voices. Bang! – Bang!

It was not yet light when the squad car arrived at the way-side station with the commandant of the district police in uniform, a plain-clothes man and two native police. A few minutes later a rail-car was signalled in from Bloemfontein to assist in the search.

The stranger, Paul Moleng, asked if he also could take part in the search, and the commandant raised his eyebrows as if to say: Who in hell are you?

'My lawyers, they will want to have a witness present,' Moleng said.

'A witness – what's this?'

'He is a relation of the accused,' the railway policeman said.

'Well, let him come.'

Paul Moleng bent over Eva. 'I am going now, but not for long.'

'Where are you going?' she said, catching her breath.

'I will be back soon. Rest a little.'

He hurried after the police and jumped on the back of the rail-car. They were signalled into the section and the little vehicle whizzed off like a bumble-bee along the tracks, its lights catching a gleam on the frosted sleepers and on bare peach trees standing along the line, their twigs white with rime.

Life began to stir at the station. Eva heard the first carts come in and the cans of fresh milk banged down with a rattle on the platform. She heard snatches of her own language. Gradually dawn spread in the angle of the sky visible to her from where she lay, but it was not the light that troubled and frightened her. Her mind was clear; the shock and dazed feeling which had been folded around her brain, as if to protect her from too sharp a sorrow, had lifted. She saw it all, and knew to every detail what had happened. In her mind she could hear even the click of the blanket pin as she had fastened it into the bundle of her lost child. No, she had not done it – they, those others, had taken him away almost as she had dreamed.

She could bear it no longer, lying there while her heart was wrenched with anguish at each sound beyond the bleak iron walls. She raised herself from the bench and came unsteadily to the entrance of the shack, holding the sides for support. With a great effort of will she straightened herself upright and the sun shone in her eyes. It was rising over the far, far hills and mountains of her homeland. She stood a long while staring into that haunting distance, now so cruel to her since she had lost it, she thought, for ever.

The police guard was looking at her in a curious way.

'I have done nothing to you,' she cried, bitter and pained. 'Why do you stare at me?'

'I am not staring.'

'Where are the others?'

'I do not know. They went to search.'

'E, to search,' she panted. 'But they left me behind. I know where to look. I know where he is – waiting there for me. Let me go.'

The policeman stretched an arm across the entrance to bar her way.

'Let me go, let me go. . . .' She struggled frantically with him. His eyes had grown large and angry, and he bit his lip, holding her back firmly. Then he saw the light go out of her face, and she became limp in his grip.

Voices were singing outside as she awoke, a gang of labourers loading bales of hides into a truck at the siding. At first there was only the song – an old chant with a slow rhythm that helped men with the heaviness of their toil – the song and she, Eva, responding to it with an aching heart. She blinked her eyelids in pain, and gazed round the hut. She remembered. A man was seated on an upturned box and a shaft of sun cut aslant his shoulder, leaving his face in shadow. She thought he was Isaiah, her husband's lame brother. He was smiling at her. Why, she thought, did he smile? There was something inexpressibly reassuring about that dark face and the shining teeth and eyes, and a sob burst from her.

'Don't cry,' he said to her, and she saw it was the stranger, Paul Moleng.

'What can I do then?' she sobbed.

'You have been greatly hurt, more than a woman should. But that is at an end. Be strong now, *ausei*, more than other women.'

'I have no strength, father.'

The men from the work-gang had stopped singing and came to the entrance where they could see her. Softly but with excitement they talked among themselves. . . . 'E, she is awake now. . . .' 'What does she say?'–'No, brother, nothing, she's crying. . . .' 'Ao! and so lucky too!' 'Quiet there.'

It seemed right that they should gather on the threshold, big quiet men like members of a family, with concern in their hushed voices. She looked about for the police.

'Where are they, the police – why do they keep me here?'

'The police have gone, you are free, do you understand?' Paul Moleng said. 'There is no case, that is all. And today the train when it comes will take you back there, home.' He jerked his thumb over one shoulder at the hills of Basutoland to the East.

She watched him, speechless, while he leaned forward and stirred some hot brew in a tin set on the ashes of the fire. The men outside seemed to draw away, letting the sunlight flood in.

'Yes, I have your ticket,' Paul Moleng went on comfortably. 'Tomorrow you will be back in Wepener, and the bus will take you home. There you will raise your child carefully. Raise him for tomorrow.'

From a corner of the shack there came a snickering and then a thin cry. The men outside had stopped murmuring and not a sound came from them. The stranger bent over his open suitcase and lifted out a bundle in a striped blanket. 'There, he is awake,' he said.

'Awake now . . .' a voice repeated outside. 'Ehe, she knows. . . .'

THE WHOLE OF LIFE

Mogamat said again: 'The white people are a lot of ——y swine!'

'Ai! Shut your mouth – scum.' One of the three old coloured women sitting on a bench aslant the fire turned round and made a face at Mogamat. The drink in him was beginning to weaken his restraints. There were two white people in the room but he was not thinking of them, he was thinking of the 'mense' in general. Like a thing he could feel they sprawled over his life; leaned against him outside the dark alleys and squashed his self-respect. Their blood ran in his veins and their sneer was written up big in the town on signs – No coloureds; – need not apply; – not admitted; whites only. He had a voice for the 'mense', a whine; he had a flicker in the eyes for them and a quick touch of his cap as a gesture. At times he snarled back as if the hairs were up along his spine, or perhaps drink would drive away the gloom in his mind. The strong doctored sherry heated his face: his natural feelings welled up against the barriers of habit and began to pour out.

Mogamat sat on a coffin. Few people would have a coffin ready before their time came, and they were the thrifty, settled type. He was young and his poverty so stark that the long box with metal handles and a solid oak lid was queer lying there in the slum room. Firelight shone on the three old women sitting side by side and on a tattered armchair with broken springs left politely for the use of the white people. Mogamat had no qualms resting there on the death-coffer. He had often carried it through the streets in funeral procession. Then he wore a red fez and walked quickly with five other pall-bearers in the Cape Malay custom. Such funerals were never stopped. The heavy traffic of the streets halted a moment to let them go by and the police saw them pass without curiosity. They were not carrying a corpse; the coffin was packed usually with sherry bottles and cheap brandy and screws of dagga to keep the old smokers fuddled and send young ones fighting crazy.

But Mogamat had quarrelled with the gang. He was afraid and sat there shaken now and then by a drunken shudder.

Over the fire which crackled in a raised hearth some large pots of water were steaming and the three women kept poking at the ashes and adding one piece of firewood after another. A drop of rainwater seeping down the chimney hissed in the coals. The old women then thought of the dreary night outside and drew their shawls closer round themselves. They were secretly excited and each of them had a sweet and prickling pain in her heart. The smell of ether and iodoform which rose above the stench of the room stirred them like incense at a mosque door. It did not remind them of prayer or death or love, but of life.

'Aaaaaaaah! aaaaaaah! Dear God!' The heart-piercing agonised cry came from a girl lying on the bed. Her last words sank away in her throat. The old women twisted their eyes towards her without turning their heads. All over the big, creaking tenement building the noises of habitation came to a stop.

'The white people . . .' Mogamat started in a shaking voice.

'Hista!' The same old woman cut him short.

'There, there, dear, it will all be over before long.' The deep, almost bass voice of Salvation Army nurse Jolivet soothed the girl. With her eyes closed she rolled her head on the evil-smelling pillow. Then, with a low trembling sigh she looked up into Nurse Jolivet's face and tried to smile.

'Where's my husband – where's Mogamat?'

'He's here, little one.'

'Tell him to fetch the doctor.' There was a slight foam on her lips as she ground out the words once more.

'Doctor is here, dear.' The girl made an effort to concentrate her gaze on the white man. She had small pretty features and a smooth forehead set in jet-black curls. Her pupils were narrowed down to dots, giving her eyes a petrified look. And her skin, once a satiny brown, was dull as wet leather.

'You are doing well,' Dr Bergson said. He felt her pulse and stroked her forehead with his hand. The slum room smelt of vermin and dirt. It was a damp odour, tinged with stale liquor, smoke and sluggish drains, that clung to walls and garments. A boarded-up window let in a little cold air through cracks and broken panes. The girl was struggling with her racked nerves and heart against it all, against long under-feeding and anxiety and lastly against the cruel duration of a difficult birth. She was quiet for a while.

Nurse Jolivet looked down at her with eyelids half closed, and with a slight shrug she bent to tuck her arms under the blanket. She could not stop to think of the awful purpose behind each life. And having so much faith and so little power, she would never understand the part God permitted her to play in the everlasting swing between living and dying.

71

'You should be in a ward, God bless you!' she said loud enough for the doctor to hear. And turning to him with an apologetic smile she added: 'That's the truth.'

'If there *was* a ward with a single vacant bed for a coloured in the whole of Cape Town,' he said.

'Perhaps . . .'

'No, I can't do anything about it, I really can't.'

She became afraid. Dr Bergson was buttoning up his overcoat to leave. It was not the danger to herself that she feared. Night after night her stout figure under a black cape moved through the half-lit streets of District Six where the police carried loaded revolvers and men did not walk alone. But she had that fear always when the great burden of life was placed suddenly in her sole care. It was a critical case.

'I am coming back.' Dr Bergson paused at the door. 'There are still a few hours.'

The look she fixed on him was desperate and the lamp shook slightly in her hand. So he made the promise. He would try to get an ambulance sent. It was hopeless but he would try; and in any case he would be back about twelve.

The door closing behind Dr Bergson muffled the sounds from the corridor. The thoughts of all in the room had hung on him, and now he had gone it was as if the centre-post had been knocked out.

'They want to put Julyga in hospital,' one of the old women whispered. The others nodded rapidly. They pursed up their lips and one after another glanced doubtfully at the white woman. Nurse Jolivet felt the tension. She had to busy herself and tried to make the patient comfortable. She began to pace the room. Her legs ached and she was weary but would not sit in the grotesque armchair for fear of fleas and other vermin. The restless scuffling of the old women's feet began to annoy her. She went calmly over to the fire. 'Keep the water nice and hot,' she said cheerfully.

'Ooh ja, Sister.'

'How have you been keeping since last winter, Mrs Paulse?'

'No, Sister, I couldn't really complain.' The old woman clucked and smiled with joy. The nurse's remembrance suddenly broadened her pinched life.

'And how's Sister so long?'

'Not so bad thank you, Mrs Paulse. Work keeps me too busy to think of being ill.'

They all worked as busily as that but liked to think they were important enough to have their ailments too. Mrs Paulse tugged at the nurse's cape and whispered: 'Is Julyga bad then?'

'No-o, she's normal.'

There was something official and cold and distant about the word 'normal', as though it had the smell of disinfectants and a taste of ether.

'Hospitaal?' Mrs Paulse lingered on the word, wrinkling her brows.

The sound of footsteps came from the corridor beyond the cracked door, many steps of boots and a padding of rubber soles. They drew nearer towards the room. And then they paused. Mogamat was slouched on the coffin with his head sunk on his chest. While the doctor was in the room he had felt a dull sense of safety. As long as Dr Bergson was there – the tall stooping white man with his red nose and hollow, sad eyes – there was not an enemy, not a gang, who would molest him. Men in the heat of a brawl put up their

73   c*

knives when that awesome person came among them striding springily, one who knew many secrets and kept them. Mogamat leaned down through force of habit and felt under his trouser leg. His knife was still there, tucked in the thick dirty stocking. He might need it now the doctor had gone. The room felt colder. He pulled the jacket lapels over his chest and his eyes darted around, coming back each time to the door. As soon as he heard the footsteps he seemed to know who was there. The pause brought on another shudder. He pressed his back against the wall and waited, terror-stricken.

The door opened and five young men came in quietly. Mogamat watched them furtively under his eyebrows as they grouped themselves round him. He heard a sharp whisper from one of the old women and saw them hunch their backs, turning their faces to the fire. They also knew who had come in. Julyga was rocking her head on the pillow.

'Stand up, Mogamat,' the leader said.

'Why should I? I am finished with you. I told you I don't belong no more.'

One of them laughed. 'You are drunk.'

'I'm not drunk. Go away, take the coffin with you – there are "mense" here.'

They looked round without interest at Nurse Jolivet.

'Did you know Willie Abels got ten years today?'

'Yes, I heard. You thought he was getting the rope,' Mogamat's eyes flickered from one face to another to see the effect of his reply. He winced.

'You will not be so lucky, Mogamat. You tell the dieners once, not twice.'

'You lie! I never told the police nothing. Was I there, eh?

74

– Did I give evidence in the case against Willie?'

'No, maybe you sent to the back door, Mogamat, just tipped them off.'

'Lie! Blerry f—— lie!' His voice rose shrilly as an animal that already feels the knife. The gang rated life cheap. The leader stretched out a hand slowly and gave Mogamat a deliberate slap across the face. Again he struck sharply with the back of his hand and poised for a third blow.

'Leave me alone, Carels,' Mogamat whined. 'What do you want here, a fight?' His fingers were trembling to grasp the knife but he saw the others were ready. Their knives were under their coats or in their sleeves easy to hand.

Nurse Jolivet walked calmly between them and they gave way to her. 'Boys,' she said in her deep, sympathetic voice, 'no fighting and quarrelling here. Out you go now please. I can't have the little mother frightened.'

Carels laid a hand on Mogamet and jerked his head towards the door. 'Kom!'

Terrified, the husband looked wildly at Nurse Jolivet and held back. The three old women had taken the courage to turn round and stare.

'Kom!' the command was hissed out louder.

'Aaaaaaah! God! God! aaaaah.' The cry from the bed froze their blood.

'Swines!' Mogamat clutched his chest with frantic hands and tore open his shirt as if his girl-wife's pain had shot through him too. Nurse Jolivet was quickly at Julyga's side and the girl gripped her hands so tightly that her nails went blue. Slowly she rolled her head over until she was glaring at the gang-men.

'Leave my man here. Go – clear out. Leave him! I'll kill you, I say.'

'Be still, dear. They'll be going,' the nurse said.

Mrs Paulse rose from the bench and her two cronies followed her. A new fierce light shone in her faded eyes. The three advanced menacingly and the terrible instinct of motherhood was roused in them to the full. They would have thrown themselves on a mad dog or torn out an armed man's eyes. The cry of the girl had gone into the blood and muscle and one of their deepest being and without a word they had risen as if the tiny body fighting for the right to exist lay in their own laps. In an instant they shed the fear distilled like a plague in the area by the gangs. Seeing their furious advance, the young men backed away, then retreated to the door and disappeared.

The victory of the old women was swift and they were carried away by a sense of their power and importance. There was an imperceptible swagger in the manner they walked back to the bench.

'Ah, the gutters are not wide enough to carry off that muck,' Mrs Paulse said, showing the whites of her eyes in a sideways glance. 'We need a strong broom to sweep out the whole dump.'

'And we could do it too! Look how they ran.'

'They're good enough to stop people alone in an alley; rob the wages of factory girls Friday nights,' Mrs Paulse said in disgust.

'I seen it too, and you can't do nothing.'

'They broke the windows in Mrs Januarie's room and smashed the furniture because she stood up for her son against Carels.'

Mrs Paulse sat down and heaved a sigh.

'They wouldn't do that to us,' said one of the others.

'No, this is another matter, a woman's business.'

76

'Still, I hope they don't remember us.'

'Aai, ai.'

The three sat there thinking a shade anxiously of their homes. Girls in the factories and decent young men who worked, some of them married. The grandchildren were in from the streets now, all crowded under the blankets fast asleep. The old women did not want revenge or spite to fall there.

A minute later the gang leader Carels slipped back stealthily and sat in the far corner. It sent a cold thrill through them but they made no move. Why look for trouble; it was enough to have chased out the gang. Julyga could not see him, the firelight glittering in her eyes as she panted.

Mogamat hunched his back at the sight of Carels. So that was the game, he thought, trembling; his enemy would wait like a cat fooling a mouse. And yet the old women there made him feel a little safer. He reached down behind the coffin and pulled up a bottle of cloudy sherry. Throwing back his head he took a long pull. His glance strayed again in fascination to the man in the corner. Carels was motionless and kept his eyes cast down. A strange calm settled over the tenement. Life was plunging down into the fertile depths of sleep. The heads of the three old women began to nod; the only movements in the room were the slow pacing of Nurse Jolivet and Mogamat's handling of the bottle.

Julyga asked faintly again after a long time if the doctor had come.

'He went out a little time back, dear, but he will soon be here.'

'Sister, Sister – am I going to die?'

'No, of course not. Doctor thinks it will be a normal birth – a bit difficult, but you are a brave girl and nothing can happen.'

'And the little one?'

'Yes, we are only waiting for him.'

'For him? Oh no. I wanted a girl.'

'For her. . . .' There was a momentary glimmer of joy in the girl's face as the picture formed in her mind. Her breathing was uneven, broken by fluttering sobs.

'You want to take me to hospital. I heard.'

'It will be comfortable' – she looked at the soiled and malodorous bedclothes. 'It is better for a young mother in a home. Not a hospital, a maternity home.'

'I don't want to die!'

'You don't have to worry, child. You are doing well, the doctor said so.'

'I want to hold my little baby. I want her alive by my heart.'

'Yes, yes, she is on the way, dear.'

Mogamat dropped a bottle and it smashed on the brick floor. He got stupidly to his feet. The women watched him lurch across the room. He climbed in the bed beside Julyga and turned his face to the wall. In a minute his drunken, regular snores cut the silence.

'The filthy wash-rag,' Mrs Paulse growled.

'Street rubbish!'

'Rag!'

They bent towards the fire again, shaking their heads. The firewood was getting low. Nurse Jolivet heard footsteps in the corridor which she recognised. She went to the door and let in Dr Bergson. One glance in those tired eyes and she said anxiously: 'No result?'

He shook his head. 'Afraid not. Something might be done tomorrow.'

'It will be too late then.'

'One cannot say.' The light from the fire and the oil lamp near the bed shed a yellow wavering gleam. The doctor came forward and regarded Mogamat without a movement of a muscle. His power among the people and their devotion to him lay in a deep understanding. He knew and accepted them as they were, even when his heart rebelled. What example he could set and what lead they could follow were ringed round by their bitter desperation. He helped Julyga into an easier position and felt the little living form under the flesh.

'Soon,' he said, glancing at the nurse.

The girl's muscles convulsed and her spine arched. Again came those penetrating, shrill cries that made a hundred hearts in the reeking old building pause an instant. Mogamat rolled over in his stupor and flung an arm round his young wife's neck. Dr Bergson was considering the appropriate moment for an anæsthetic and a sudden fury seized him at the interruption.

'Away with him!' he rapped out. The three old women and Nurse Jolivet moved the bed quickly from the wall and dragged Mogamat to the floor. They trailed him across the room. Carels was standing there grinning and he had the lid of the coffin open in his hands.

'Throw him in,' Carels said. 'Let him cool down safe and happy.'

Though they had no good thought for Carels the gang leader, their rage was focused at that instant on the helpless father. They let him drop into the coffin and he fell with a clinking rattle. The coffin held a layer of liquor bottles.

Carels let down the lid and it rested slightly askew on Mogamat who was stretched with one arm hanging out of the coffin and part of his deathly pale face and a shock of long black hair visible. The split toe of a rubber sand-shoe also poked from under the lid.

The old women were nervous. They did not like to see a live man there in a coffin. True, he needed to be punished, yet there was a sense of awe and fate about a man being flung with five toes in the grave and his enemy laughing over him.

Their thoughts were drawn away by the commotion round Julyga. A clamminess came on dry hands and their breath was caught up short as they watched the doctor with a lamp strapped to his forehead shooting the beam this way and that in his quick movements. Mrs Paulse went to stoke up the fire and throw on some of the last wood left in the heap. In the bottom of her stomach was a twist of curdling pain, and her fellow-feeling speeded up the drumming of her heart. Her face burned. She saw the door open and two of the young men who had been there earlier dart in.

'Dieners!'

Carels, their leader, jumped to his feet and beckoned to them. He prised open the rickety window and climbed out, followed by the others in quick succession. It was all over in a breath. Mrs Paulse left the fire and walked solidly across to close the door and then the window through which a chilly draught crept. The police were on the way. She was scared and angry thinking of them. Why could the room not be left that night in peace? At first her eyes caught the gleam of a flashlight in the crack along the threshold and instantly a heavy banging shook the old panels. Four uniformed police and a plain-clothes man pushed in.

Dr Bergson turned like a soldier caught in an ambush. His eyes were wide and staring, resentful of the noisy interruption. The lamp on his forehead picked out an amazed expression on the face of the police sergeant.

'I am Dr Bergson. This is a dangerous operation. What have you come for?'

The sergeant cleared his throat and swallowed. He had come to interrogate one Mogamat and search the premises for illegal drink and dagga.

'Can't you realise – a life is in danger, two lives, and I won't allow you here!'

The policeman understood and preferred to be out of such a situation. At any time he would come back. But the plainclothes man whispered to him and he changed his mind.

'I should have a look round first,' he said.

Dr Bergson drew in a hissing breath. 'Duty, of course. Very well. There's your man, one Mogamat I understand. As you can see, he's already in his coffin.'

One of the younger constables clipped and unclipped his revolver holster nervously. He was anxious to go and began moving towards the door; the others were following him. The detective was suspicious. After hesitating too, he came back to the coffin. It seemed to Dr Bergson that something extraordinary was happening. It did not concern him – that was his motto in the silent war of the slums. It did not concern him. And here he was, vitally interested. There were the two on the bed – both children after all – whose lives he was fighting for. The fight would not end that night. Months of struggle would follow, for food, warmth, shelter, while the husband was ground through the pulp-mills of the courts and prisons. Perhaps it was coming to him, perhaps he would be better off behind bars – that was not the point. The others needed him. Given a day or two to recover, he might clear himself with the police.

The detective bent to lay his hand on the coffin lid.

'One moment,' Dr Bergson said. 'Do you wish to examine the body?'

Puzzled, the official looked up and replied that it was not his job. 'I'm not a doctor.'

'I am,' said Dr Bergson. 'I have had no time to form any conclusion. But——' he spoke coldly – 'the possibilities are smallpox or Asiatic cholera.'

The plain-clothes man drew back. In a life of risks, this was not one his duties called on him to accept. Mrs Paulse watched the police go out one by one through the door; tall, strongly-built young men, the dark-blue greatcoats stretched neatly across their square shoulders and sprinkled with raindrops. The detective was the last to go. He stood a moment holding the half-closed door and looked back. The firelight caught on his glasses. Then the door slammed sharply.

With the noise, Mogamat rolled over and sent the coffin lid slithering to the floor. Mrs Paulse held her breath. The sounds of footsteps faded and silence fell on the shambling tenement. All the time she had stood with a piece of firewood in her hand. Her fingers slowly and involuntarily relaxed until the wood dropped with a rattle on the tin sheet in which the fire ashes collected.

That last little clatter was startling, making her two companions jump in their seat. Dr Bergson whipped round angrily. 'Quiet! Damn it!'

'There I go. It's my fault, Doctor.' Her eyes glistened as she looked at the doctor's strained face. His gloves were discoloured. The struggle was on.

The three old women waited together on the bench while the fire steadily burned up and the wood began to crackle merrily, shooting out sparks on the floor and radiating a warm light to the corners of the room. The walls seemed slowly to dissolve in glowing colours and the patches of damp to creep away.

Nurse Jolivet stood up. There was a small pale-brown thing in her hands. She turned it over and it gave a feeble cry. Mrs Paulse flung her apron over her head. An inexpressible gladness crept through her breast and she could not move or speak or weep.

They washed it and wrapped it tenderly. Dr Bergson went out silently like a tall, sad ghost, fastening the door behind him; they scarcely noticed him go. Mogamat was still sleeping. When Julyga awoke the four women smiled as they put the little boy in her arms. She knew then. They told her, but it mattered nothing that it was not a girl as she had wished. She knew he was alive because she felt him stirring strongly against her. He was alive, the world had waited and suffered for his coming. He seemed to be the whole of life.

He came out of the shadow of the bush path and blinked in the sun. The clearing was scattered with refuse and tufts of dry marsh-grass struggling to keep a foothold against the bush. The sun beat on his head but he was listening and took no notice of the heat and of the flies that buzzed up at any slight movement. His face hardened and he ran his tongue quickly over his full, strong lips. He could hear them singing, children singing a hymn tune on a Sunday morning. Which direction did the voices come from?

The willow-bush stretched on for miles, criss-crossed by a thousand paths. One minute you were hidden in the dense acrid-smelling foliage, your footsteps muffled in soft white sand; the next, you were in the midst of a shanty cluster. Thousands of shanties and pondokkies grew overnight with the swiftness of a malignant fungus in the bush. They were the homes of the people flocking like migrant birds, with an urgent necessity, to the city. Once the land had been gleaming white dunes until the willow-bush crept over it and bound down the moving sand and shut out the sea-haze and the great blue outline of Table Mountain anchored in sky-space above the city. Now the shanty-clusters brought a half-wild life into the bush. The axe was heard; women laughed and hens clucked; men shouted to one another over the tree-tops.

He remembered how the police sometimes came; they tramped along the maze of sand-paths at night carrying flashlights, keeping together in parties of a hundred or more with reinforcements waiting beside the nearest roads. Next day the shanty-dwellers would set their life in order again, talking with a low hum of voices, cursing. Sometimes a song would start, a song of lamenting, and among those who joined in would be a few with tear-brimmed eyes.

On that Sunday morning Benjamin Segode listened to a different kind of song, a Christmas hymn of rejoicing. He had been brought up a Christian at a Mission in Basutoland. His father was a churchwarden and people said there was no one for a week's journey who could preach like him. Benjamin had saddened his father, asking why he, the best preacher in Mafeteng, swept the church floor while the white missionary was up in the pulpit and could hardly make himself understood. His father had said: 'God's will is not always plain for a boy to see.' Benjamin had left Basutoland and never returned. Though he remembered his father's sorrowing voice and resigned expression of face and hands, he had not stopped asking questions. His Sesotho Bible lay, carefully wrapped, in the bottom of his tin box and he felt its presence there like his father's voice, reproachful, full of distant music.

He wiped his face with a red handkerchief before he pushed aside the foliage and went on. He walked slowly, picked a leaf involuntarily and bit it, tasting the sharp, astringent juice. The veins pulsed in his neck and anger was rising in his wide, upward-slanting eyes. He had a mouth turned up at the corners too so that in his utmost temper there would still remain the shadowy semblance of a smile.

The singing came to him more distinctly as he pushed on with muffled steps along the path. Children's voices, not in his language but in Afrikaans, the language of the whiteman. That was what he disliked and suspected.

Then he was out in a big clearing. Six or seven dwellings sprawled among a few tall trees. Close by was the pondokkie of a wood-hawker opening on a sandy yard where he kept his two donkeys, stacks of cut wood, chopping-blocks and everywhere untidy heaps of wood chips, bark, refuse. The donkeys stood in the sun on three legs, leaning their necks over the fence. The wood-hawker himself was slouched asleep against his pondokkie wall while his wife stooped over a washing-tub full of soapsuds. Neither took any notice of the singers. Benjamin Segode looked at them carefully and counted the children – twenty or more of them sitting and standing in a little circle under the shade of a large willow. The tree grew at the far corner of the wood-hawker's yard and trailed its ragged branches over two more shanties standing back to back on the other side of the fence. The singing was led by a pretty white girl of fourteen or fifteen. She stood with her back to the tree, Bible in hand, and sunlight filtering through the leaves made bright moving dots on her white cotton dress and her blonde hair braided in two plaits over her shoulders.

Benjamin stood at the edge of the bush. None of them had seen him.

> *'O die vrolike, o die salige*
> *Vredebringende Kersfeestyd. . . .'*

– the child voices sang with a lilt –

> 'O Joyful and blessed, peace-bringing Christmastide . . .
> Holy choirs of angels sing the happy news . . .'

He walked out towards the woman at the wash-tub until his shadow fell across the soapsuds and she looked up quickly.

'Dumela,' he said quietly.

'Dumela, Segode,' she greeted him, smiling. Then she caught the look in his eye and glanced across, suddenly scared, to where her husband dozed in the sun.

'Is there trouble?' she asked in a low voice.

'You should know.' His gaze turned to the girl and her Sunday school.

She did not follow his meaning. 'Here is Benjamin Segode,' she sang out to her husband. The sleeping man stirred and settled back, his hat pushed still farther over his face.

'Are your children there too?' Benjamin jerked his head towards the big tree. She was a little alarmed by the question and stood with the soapy water falling in drops off her fingers. Then she nodded. 'My children and the other children.'

'How can you sell them – are they cattle?'

'I do not sell my own children. Segode, what are you saying?'

She dried her hands on her apron, looking away from him, and walked with heavy steps to the pondokkie. 'Wake up.' She touched her husband on the shoulder. 'Here is a visitor.'

The wood-seller sat up and yawned.

'Ho, Segode!' he held out a hand genially. 'Dumela, brother.'

'Dumela.'

'What brings us the good luck of this visit, Mr Secretary?'

Benjamin warmed to the man's good-natured manner.

He would have liked to squat at his side and smoke a cigarette with him there in the sun. But he stood back unbending.

'Do your eyes see what mine do?' he asked.

'Brother, I think they do.'

'That?' And he pointed expressively with his middle finger at the circle of children and the white girl at the far end of the yard beyond the donkeys.

The wood-seller stood up. 'Is there anything against that?' He screwed up the corners of his eyes.

'You must answer for yourself,' Benjamin said, feeling the heat and indignation rising up again in his veins. The woman had gone round to the other side of the pondokkie and he could hear her voice in a soft cooing tone call to someone out of sight. 'Ay, here is our Vigilance secretary, Benjamin Segode.' Voices answered from the bush, quietly, like the note of the Cape robin.

'It keeps the children out of mischief and no harm is done,' the wood-hawker said in a conciliating manner.

'You gave her permission to teach in your yard?'

The man nodded and tried to smile although he could see the secretary had brought a flame of anger to singe him.

'No – you cut wood all day,' Benjamin said, 'and you have a heart of wood and a brain of wood. Are you all the same – does your wife have soapy water in her veins? No harm is done! You hand over to them the children of our people; you, Washington Mahleke, sell your own flesh and blood for a morning on your back in the sun!'

'Hai, Segode!' the wood-seller cut in.

'Why can't you keep them out of mischief yourselves? Teach them to be true men and girls, teach them the songs of our race that are forgotten here in this stinking marsh. Teach them to rise up out of the mud!'

88

The wood-seller tugged his beard nervously. The secretary was a younger man than he and, by rights, had no business to give him such a rating. But he drew a deep breath and said bitterly: 'There is some truth in what you say, Segode.'

Benjamin waited in silence until their eyes met. He hated the indolence of people who could forget everything in a song or could dance the moon down into the gleaming ocean, dreaming of a full life, and of friendship and peace until the sun woke them up in the naked helplessness of their poverty. He saw his words had shaken Washington Mahleke and touched a hidden sore. Again he mopped his face with the red handkerchief and walked over to the Sunday-school circle. The dry twigs cracked under his boots. The children looked round to see who came, gladly letting their attention wander from the lesson. They had stopped singing and the white girl was reading to them from the Bible. Most of them were pure blacks but there were a few Cape Coloured children among them and all could understand the language they spoke, which was Afrikaans. The girl was reading in Afrikaans and held open her Bible in both hands. A ray of sunlight shone through the stray wisps of her blonde hair on the pages of the Book. She paused, looking at Benjamin Segode with her bright greenish eyes.

'Go on,' he said.

She was reading from Genesis the story of the disinheriting of Ishmael, son of the Egyptian bondwoman.

' "And Sarah saw the son of Hagar the Egyptian, which she had born unto Abraham, mocking." '

She looked up from the page and noticed the sinister smile of the black man.

'Go on,' Segode repeated.

' "Wherefore she said to Abraham: 'Cast out this bondwoman and her son, for the son of this bondwoman shall not be heir with my son, even with Isaac.' " '

The girl's lips quivered and she could not read further. Benjamin Segode stepped between the sitting children and approached her. She had turned paler and watched him with a fixed look. He could see now she had brown flecks in the green of her eyes. They were firm, steady eyes, wide open and glistening. Involuntarily she had pressed the open Book against her bosom and waited, standing her ground.

'Good morning – and who sent you here to do this?' he said in English.

'I'm sorry, I don't speak that language.'

He repeated his words in Afrikaans with the thick overtone of a Basuto accent. He knew five languages and the babel of the new slums was easy to him. The girl frowned in the effort to decide whether she should answer a black man's questions. Then she said honestly: 'The Dominie sent me.'

'What is your name?'

'Angelina du Preez.'

'So the Dominie sends you and you come here alone to preach to the heathens. Why doesn't he come himself?'

'He is too busy – he has to preach to the white people at three services and baptize and teach the Catechism.'

'He's not afraid to come here?'

She flushed. 'No, he is not afraid.'

'He marks the Book for you and the chapters you must read and the hymns to sing?'

'Yes.'

'And you believe in God and Jesus Christ and the Saints?'

She frowned again and decided not to answer. The strange, flickering smile of the man was beginning to freeze her.

Black people were coming from all sides as if there were no reason for coming but simply a chance they happened along that way. Men with a jacket hung on one shoulder, a woman hitching up a baby in the blanket on her back, older children with long bare legs and bare feet shuffling in a half-dance through the sand. They all stopped in different groups when they were some way off and seemed to be speaking to one another, yet she felt they were watching her, listening to her every word. She was a long way, more than a mile, more than half an hour's walk through the bush on heavy sand-paths to the nearest whiteman's house. She could scream and her voice would be lost in the willows.

'Does the Dominie also give you sweets for the children?' Benjamin asked her.

'No.' Her face clouded with bitter resentment at the unjust question. 'I buy sweets for them out of my own pocket money.'

He turned to the children. 'Do you like sweets on a Sunday morning?'

They did not answer but lowered their big wondering eyes to avoid his sneering look. They loved their little teacher and were troubled and a little panic-stricken at the manner and tone of the powerful secretary.

'Let me see your Book?' He waited to receive it. But she was suspicious and pressed it still tighter to her as if to protect it with her life.

'Why are you afraid to let me see it – is it not a good Book?'

'Yes, it's the one and only Book.'

Slowly and reluctantly she yielded up the Bible and he took it in both hands with the traditional African courtesy. To take anything with one hand was an affront to the giver.

He saw it was marked in a number of places with small pieces of black ribbon, but he did not trouble to see what the Dutch Reformed minister had set for reading. It was easy to find in the great Book he had been brought up on a justification, or at least a point of argument, for almost anything – for peace as well as for violence and treachery, for avarice and deceit and hatred, or for love and goodness. He knew how oppression could be sanctified as the curse of God on Ham or the casting out of the sons of Ishmael and the choosing of Israel. It was not honest, it was not the spirit of the Book; but it was done. Benjamin closed the pages and held it flat between the palms of his hands. It was a finely-printed Bible bound in black American cloth with the paper edges tinted red.

'Juffrou du Preez, we black people know this book – do you understand? We have had it for more than a hundred years, two hundred. It is full of good, it is written in a way that the heart of a man understands. But I say we should put it away for a time. I mean that we do not accept it from you. Do you hear? We do not believe you, we do not trust you – you, little girl, and your Dominies and your rich men and your soldiers and policemen. When we are equal and free we will take up the Bible again. Then we will be happy with it and no one will make us afraid. Is that understood?'

He raised his voice and she pressed her back against the tree with a sense of terror, watching him, and beyond him the hundreds of black people gradually closing up.

'Is it understood?' he demanded again.

'I don't understand. I have done nothing wrong.'

'No, Juffrou du Preez'– he gave a short deep laugh –'you have done right, by your own people. You have come here to capture our children as slaves.'

'Aah, that is a terrible thing to say. It is not true, I vow and swear it is not true.'

'Well, we have had enough. But your Dominie sends you to preach your laws.'

'I have preached no laws.'

'You think you are above us and can talk down to our children because your white Parliament has passed a hundred Acts to lower us.'

'That is politics, and I know nothing about it. I have never heard of such Acts or talked about them. If you say false things before these children, then I deny them and God is my only witness of the truth.'

She was white-faced and the pink had drained even out of her lips. But she spoke back at him with a desperate courage, putting him into a rage.

'The truth, the truth,' he shouted contemptuously. 'Every lie is the truth for your kind. You twist everything to suit yourselves.'

Somebody laughed in the crowd behind him, and from the menace in that laugh she felt her knees grow soft and tremble.

Benjamin Segode handed back the Bible.

'*Nou vat jou Boek en trek* (take your Bible and clear out),' he said in a controlled voice. She stood a moment pressing it to her thudding heart.

'*Trek, trek!*' he shouted.

And without knowing what she was doing, she began to run. A little figure in white in the gleaming sunlight, her blonde hair-braids tied with white ribbons flying out behind her and the Bible, black and red, clutched under one arm. The people in the wood-hawker's yard parted to let her go. She ran past the iron wash-tub swimming with soap-suds and past the wood-hawker himself at his door with a slender home-made pipe between his teeth.

In a few seconds she was out of the yard and had plunged down one of the sandy paths into the tunnel of the bush. There she saw a single black man coming her way, and in her panic she ran on straight towards him, almost into his arms. Surprised, he stepped aside, pushing into the wall of leaves, to let her pass. Her feet sank deep into the sand at each step, and running was like the cloying horror of a nightmare.

Angelina du Preez did not know how long or how far she had run when she came to a stop. There was a taste of blood in her throat and her heart was knocking and jolting as if it would leap out of her breast. It was the first time she had ever felt like that. Her legs were weak and heavy almost as though detached from her body. At first she listened for anyone who might be following her. There was no sound except the faint crackle of bush seeds ripening in the sun and the swish of leaves stirred by a slight eddy. That was all she could hear for a while, holding her breath; that, and the drumming in her ears. Somewhere a cock crowed; far off, out of sight, an aeroplane hummed in the sky. She longed just to catch sight of it, but the strip of sky above the path was narrow and gave her no view. She could not tell where she was or which way she should now go to get back on the tarmac road, the cars passing and the houses of white people. She changed her Bible into the other hand, thinking what to do.

Trying to fix her bearings, she was certain of one thing alone – the direction from which she had run. Should she continue and trust to chance? But doing so, she might stumble upon more bunches of unknown, hostile pondokkies; she might encounter a skolly gangster drunk and treacherous on the lonely bush path. It was cowardly to hold such fears, and she tried to fight them down in her mind. 'God help me, Lord God help me,' she prayed.

In that vague, rustling emptiness with every bush watching her and maybe concealing something, she had nothing to grip on to, nothing but the thought of the little children she had come to teach and to know. Sunday after Sunday she had found them waiting for her. Surely they had grown to love her in their own way and no harm would come to her among them. It had been a foolish and mad thing to run away from the native leader, for she had thus accepted his charge of wrong, of untruth and twisting. And in one minute of fear she had lost the children and undone the work and the first mission of her young life. How could she explain it? If she were to set right her mistake she must go back and face the black people, whatever the consequences, whatever the danger and threat to her life itself. There was no other way. 'O Lord God, help me,' she prayed.

The way back was plain to find. She simply turned and followed the path, going neither to right nor left. But at each step, at each sound from the bush, her courage sagged. Then, after what seemed a long time, she heard a murmur of human voices somewhere ahead, and she had to stop to let her heart slow down. The voices became louder as she continued.

At last she reached the edge of the clearing near the wood-seller's fenced-in yard and peered out from among the foliage. Where she had taken her Sunday school class, under the same sheltering tree, the secretary was holding a meeting. He spoke slowly and expressively in a language she did not understand and hundreds of people in the yard responded to him with rumbling voices or with a sigh. They had their backs to her. The native leader had turned her cowardly running away into a success for himself. On the edge of the crowd were the children, her children. They were not listening, but seemed drawn by the stir and passion among their elders.

She walked out across the sand into the full sunlight. They noticed her at once. A murmur came from them and hundreds of dark faces turned towards her. The secretary stopped in the middle of his speech. Some of the children started talking excitedly, but their elders hushed them.

She came near the children and opened her mouth, but her throat was dry and no sound emerged. Again she tried and said huskily: 'Children, I have one more thing to say and one hymn to sing with you before I go today. . . .'

She did not know how to continue, and there was a silence.

Then she said: 'Will you listen to me, my children?'

A small boy hiding behind a companion piped up 'No!' A faint rustle like a deep breath rose from the crowd.

'Gracie, will you listen to me?' Angelina appealed.

A little black girl with her crimpy hair done in a dozen plaits said softly: '*Ja, my nonnatjie.*'

'No!' shouted another shrill voice.

Then one of the children picked up a wood chip and tossed it at the white girl. It grazed her sunburnt leg and left a slight scratch and a bead of blood. Another chip followed and another, until in a moment they were all pelting her as hard as they could, laughing and jeering at her. Some chips hit her and some flew past. They did not hurt her; she could not feel them. But the wound they made was deep in her breast. She stood there in the sunlight and bowed her head and began to cry.

Benjamin Segode rushed from his place at the tree and stopped the children throwing wood chips. 'Hai!' he hissed at them furiously. 'What is this – are you hooligans?'

The children shrank back among the people and the whole crowd fell quite silent. Some watched and some turned away their eyes while the white girl stood there and cried, shaken with long choking sobs, and the tears ran down her small face and dropped in the hot sand.

SAY IT WITH FLOWERS

She halted under the arcade and stood there blindly staring out into the sunlight. She was black, or more nearly a dark, dull, earth colour, a Mosuto girl, and her eyes were mindless and shallow, glittering in a blank stare.

People passed her in crowds, all moving in one direction, and she stood alone with her back to the shop window staring out and seeing nothing. She had come a long way and had stopped to gather herself against the pain that was killing her.

There was no time to lose, and she wanted to move on. She had another eighteen miles to walk, and every minute she delayed there was a greater likelihood that they would find her and take her back. But she stood there, and it was no use thinking she could move a step until she fought down the pain and took firmer possession of herself. A big swathe of bandages enfolded her head and under the chin, and her mouth was covered by a pad of cotton-wool lightly tied. From a cord round her neck hung a small oval medallion of the Virgin and Child. She breathed through wide quivering nostrils and her open eyes were turned in upon the one appalling spectacle of herself, of her fight for self-possession.

Her simple green blouse and black skirt were crumpled; she had pulled them on in a hurry and walked out of the hospital. At first the sheer terror of the escape had occupied her, the heavy slugging of her heart. The streets were drenched in sparkling sunshine and not a leaf stirred; the wind-frayed palms were still, smoke-plumes going up softly from the power-station into a white sky. Women and young girls were everywhere in light frocks, the buildings white in the sunlight and the Mountain carrying pockets of mauve haze in its kloofs. October, a spring morning. The people stepped lightly, talking and laughing, moving aside to pass the slowly plodding Mosuto girl with her bandaged head. Malay girls went by swinging wide skirts with a rustle of stiff petticoats. Young white women entered the tall office blocks where they worked, fresh and assured as if they had an assignation and were late on purpose.

She walked on, more slowly, and the pain caught up and accompanied her every step. When she halted under the arcade she had ceased noticing, alone with the many-armed but single agony within herself. People flocked past her going from the upper streets towards the centre of the city. Some glanced at her and stopped a moment before hurrying on. They saw the hands stiff as wood and the face dead save for the racked glittering eyes in dark rings.

When she wanted to look back the way she had come, the pain gripped at her. They would be after her to take her back to her bed in the hospital and she was terrified, but she could not go on. Not yet, not until she fought down the dark thing, the evil that was gripping her. She stood there swaying and all things slipped subtly away from her.

They had come to fetch her in the shanty-town and she had lain in a clean acid-smelling bed. The pain they took away with the prick of a needle, and she thought before she faded into sleep that she had been cured, a sense of floating on the clouds, of paradise, her head among the clouds free from pain. But she found she had not been cured. She was taken to a different place and wheeled under an X-ray machine, and afterwards an ambulance moved her to the isolation hospital. They told her not to worry, they said reassuring things to her. One among the hospital orderlies was a Mosuto like herself, and he translated what the doctor said. He did not look straight at her, repeating the white man's words. She was young, but she was ugly and flat-chested and bony and her face was dark with the shadows of suffering. No man would look at her, but when the orderly spoke and his face was averted from her she felt already half dead. She had been brought there to die.

If she died in the hospital they would take away her body and bury it in some nameless place, and she did not want that, she could not bear to think of it. She wanted to die in the shanty and be buried curled up like a child with her brow on her knees and all the other children around her in the small patch among the willows, each with a wooden cross and a pot or two of flowers. She wanted someone to look at her, someone to weep.

She felt stronger and started off again trying to walk carefully so that each step should not send through her a jarring blade of pain. It was worse where the pavement ran down steep and her feet became unsteady. On the level the going was easier. She was walking in the same direction as everybody else now, office girls and young men and business people and the kind of women who did not work but were in town for the morning and had parked their cars in the squares. The sun was on their heads as they crossed the wide streets, sun glinting on slowly-moving cars and vans and tall green buses. In the lower streets the crowds were quite large and the motor traffic had been diverted. The Mosuto girl plodded on among them all.

They began to delay her, there were so many. But when they turned and saw her they stopped laughing or talking for a moment and allowed her to pass. She was so intent on getting through. They stepped aside to let her go by, but the sense of them on all sides made her afraid. Once she was brought to a halt and she uttered a little desperate cry muffled by the bandages. A white girl swung round and her soft yellow hair flew with her movement. Her brow suddenly contracted, and gently she said: 'Shame!' A lane was opened by the gay, brightly-dressed people and the Mosuto girl went on, oppressed and dull-skinned and the mindless eyes motionless in their hollows.

At last they stopped her. There was a rope spanning the crossing and beyond it the broad open street full of sunlight, the radiance caught in the funnel of tall buildings. People everywhere, girls in wide-skirted print frocks on the balconies, young men in shirt-sleeves leaning from windows, heads against the skyline. The other side of the street was packed with people too. She could not understand it; she did not try to think what was happening. They had stopped her, that was all. Before her was the rope and a few big sun-burnt men in the khaki uniform and gold buttons and the white crash-helmets of the traffic control. They were not letting anyone through.

There was a sound of cheering from far down in the valley of the street and drum-beats and a whirl of lilting music. People craned their necks and swayed to see. The girl stared before her; she wanted to go over, to get beyond the crowd and cover some of the long walk home. Nothing else interested her. The pain was rising and sweeping in gradual waves across her senses like dark shadows in the mind's eye, but less intense than before and giving her time to recover.

A line of motor-cycle outriders came up the open street and behind them the cavalcade. It was a cavalcade of flowers, the cars and the picture-floats and old-fashioned landaus all loaded under massed banks of flowers, proteas with their pink and gold and lavender colours, white arums, poppies, wild aloes and heaths and shining eternelles. The girls were like flowers too, from a distance, white and brown girls laughing and waving back at the crowds.

The cavalcade went on and she waited only for it to end. It stood between her and the continuing of her long flight. It had arrested her when she needed all her strength to keep moving. Everything had gone past her still gaze and now she felt they would let her through. But somewhere at the top of the open street there was a commotion, and the outriders and drum-majorettes and pipe band and the moving flower pictures were rolling down again on the side of the street where the girl stood bewildered and panting like a sheep through her nose.

They came past her quite close, but she saw little, the movement and the colour and the feeling of brightness, but not the details. The words people spoke were lost on her too, and their laughter was a part of that bright hard feeling that cut into her.

Then she noticed the movement had stopped and she raised her eyes slowly. Only a few feet from her was the queen of the festival, the Flower Queen, a young girl with a fair skin, her white skirt billowing around her and a coronet of glistening artificial pearls against her dark hair. She was waving to somebody and laughing, and then she glanced along the ranks of the crowd until she saw the Mosuto girl. Their looks met and the smile faded on her lips. A moment later the procession was moving again, and the sick girl's eyes, come to life, followed the other down the street.

Someone was tossing out keepsakes of violets tied in paper ribbons, and one fell on her shoulder and slipped to her feet. She did not bend to pick it up, hardly noticing it, and a small coloured boy put it in her stiff fingers. The touch made her start. Her eyes, which had been gazing down the street after the retreating floats, fixed on the blooms and coloured ribbons that she gripped and she thought wildly and bitterly of herself going like this, fleeing across the city, to die. Tears welled suddenly and splashed down the crumpled green blouse front. For a minute she stood with her jaw sagging weakly in the bandage and the tears flooding without a sob, streaming over her cheeks or soaking away in the gauze.

The rope was moved and the crowds flowed into the open street. The girl went forward, unconsciously clutching the violets, and soon she had the way ahead of her unimpeded but for the ordinary run of traffic. There were fewer people on the foot-walks, but, as she went so slowly, she was continually being overtaken. She could think of nothing but the dazzling crown, the dark hair and blue eyes of the Flower Queen, her fair skin and white dress and the laughter welling up in her. The sight of her with her bandaged head had made the white girl's laughter die in her throat. What had she thought then – had she seen how near death was? But in a little while she would quite forget, thinking of other things, and not the way their looks had met.

'*Ausei* – sister – where are you going?' The quiet voice

103

was in her language and was like a sound in her own head. 'Are you not afraid to walk in the streets? You are not strong enough.'

'I am strong enough,' she said in a muffled voice, as if answering her own doubts, plodding heavily on and not turning.

The hospital orderly had followed her. He had left the ambulance at the kerb and was walking near her side but a little behind. He spoke to her softly, not to strike fear into her. She was killing herself. Unless he brought her back with her own consent and will, she would die.

'Are you cured yet, *ausei*? Have the white people taken away your pain and cured you?'

'They took away my pain, but they gave it back. I carry it with me. I am not cured.'

'Where do you find the strength to rise up from your bed?'

It was no mere voice in her head. She was being pursued, and now her heart was bumping strangely, and she could not control it. She stood still again, panting swiftly, and leaned against a shop window, holding her head with one hand.

'I am strong, I am strong enough,' she said, and then was silent for a little. 'That other one I saw riding there with the crown on her head like the Mother of Jesus in our Church, she could not look at me. She is living and good to look at, and she turned away. . . .' She drew her breath, waiting. 'The man of my people in the hospital, with a white coat, he spoke to me well. He, too, could not look at me. Why could they not look in my face? I am strong, that is why. They are afraid of dying. I am not afraid of death, that makes me strong . . . because I am going . . .'

'*Ausei*, you are not going to die. The man in hospital turned from you to hide his tears. He knew the pain you bear.'

'He knew he was looking at one dying.'

'No one knows that but God. I knew only how heavy it was with my sister.'

'You . . . are you the man? No.' She gazed but with blank eyes at him. He was not in his overall and was wearing dark things.

'Yes, I am the man.'

'The white one with the crown, I saw her, she turned from me too. She knew.'

'No, she hid her eyes from pity.'

'What is pity?'

'It is that one knows another's suffering.'

'Ai!' she moaned quietly, and she looked up at him, her eyes clearing.

'Sister, it is heavy with you, but still you want to live.'

She bowed her head again, knowing it was true. For all the pain and the weight on her heart, he had given her hope, and with it, fear. She whispered to herself: 'I want to live like the others, I want to live, but I am afraid.'

'Let me help you, *ausei*.'

'How can you help me?' She knew that he could, though it needed every last drop she had left from the great river which gave her life to force herself back. And now she had chosen, she stood a little longer, then turned to go with him.

NO TEA FOR THE MEMSAHIB

They sat at the long cedarwood table with their backs to the wall. Mich was in the middle and had a service revolver ready on the table near his fruit-plate. Behind him was a walled-in window. He could, if he wished, look across the room through high french windows open to the marvellous wildness of the garden. But instead he kept swivelling his eyes between the single door and his cousin Hugh, trying to be impressive. He wanted to impress Hugh, and he had a feeling it wasn't working. Hugh was bland, polite. He could just as well be dining at the Muthaiga Club in Nairobi, or in London for that matter; not here in the White Highlands. Hugh hadn't cottoned on to Africa, he showed no grip concerning the Mau-Mau emergency and he went about the farm brisk and self-assured like a young English squire, as if he owned the place – which, of course, he did. He owned every acre, every stone, every tree that was left standing on Upper Gilgit farm. That was a thing Mich could not forget. He was haggard with thinking of it.

He thought of other things meanwhile, for relief, until Everill prodded him back to his bitter worry. Then the cracks and seams spread over his face and his soul was again in torment. Everill sat on his right with her back to the wall too and facing the door. She was much more than Mich's wife and the mother of their only son Selwyn; she was the little sharp instrument in his vitals like the governor of a big, slow-running motor. He could not get up in the morning, he could not walk fast or slow or suffer from flatulence or sign his name but that he felt the needle of her pull surely but subtly regulating him. Oddly, it did not chafe him with dependence or inferiority to have her there, but gave him an extraordinary feeling of free will, which was the essence of power. In a devious way he was aware in himself of brilliant talents, surprising capabilities. Such versatile and decorative posts as Governor of the Colony or Commander of the Armed Forces were not beyond him. Evvy would always be behind him as his point of reference. He could not fail. Only she could fail. If he were ever to ride through the cloud-pillared tropical sky hurling down death on the lurking enemy, she would see his daring did not bring him to grief. She was his radar-control, his genius. Mich was feverishly imaginative and enjoyed moving among his own beliefs.

The latch of the dining-room door clicked and both Mich and Everill came to the alert. Hugh took no notice whatever. In any case, he was seated at one end of the table and would need to turn his head while the other two were facing full towards the door. Hugh simply went on staring through the french windows. Evening was coming down with greenish shifting colours, making mysterious the fantastic neglect of the garden, the oversize plants, unseasonable lilies – because no seasons ruled there at the Equator poised among the mists on the roof of Africa – and the giant night-flowering cactus blooms. The night wind was getting up with a great deep moan over the highest trees.

Mich put a hand on his revolver. Evvy did not have her gun exposed. But she kept her handbag on the table corner, in it a white-handled little automatic she had never fired, and wouldn't know how to. Owarunga, the Kikuyu house servant, came in with a pot of soup and bowls and glasses tinkling faintly on a tray as he walked. He was a small man with a big almost top-heavy head, out of which looked gently inquisitive eyes. His movements were shy and quick, not as if he were afraid of Mich and the revolver, but felt uncomfortable in the silence of the long, half-blocked-in room and wanted to get speedily outside to the kitchen where a blend of noise, dirt. smoke and children made his life tolerable. He allowed himself the mere fraction of a glance at the Bwana Hugh before going out. He knew Hugh was the real owner and master and had seen something of him during the day, but was still sizing him up. After a few nights sleeping and brooding he would have formed not an opinion, but an attitude regarding this man. And the attitude would seep and spread down among the people like a new rain on the manyattas. A few drops of water for some far-off, unhurried harvest.

The door clicked again behind Owarunga, and Mich drummed a few times on the table with his finger-tips. He was waiting to catch Hugh's eye, and when he did his face had about it a kind of trembling resolution.

'One day I'll have to fill him with lead. I don't want to – he's not a bad little devil. But it's one of those things. . . .' He pursed his lips together. 'One of those things you can't get away from.'

'Ah, yes,' Hugh said, gazing once more through the windows into the last afterglow of the day. Far off through gaps between the trees was the purpling horizon. From the edge of the lawn on a clear day you could see the snow peak of Mount Kenya marvellously serene aloft the vast contortions of Africa's spine. Such skies were not frequent. He would love to ask a thousand questions and hear tales, queer or heroic, to bring close the dark, slow pulse of the land so he could feel and respond to it through his own sensibility. But with Mich and Evvy he came up against a blank, a curious emptiness he was unable to get past. They could be no link to the Africa he wished to touch.

So he had taken Owarunga when the little house servant was off duty and Mich and Evvy had their customary afternoon sleep. Taking Owarunga meant taking five, or was it seven, half-naked, snotty-nosed little boys as well. They made a hushed, shifting procession first along the district road that traversed the farm and then cutting up a lumber track to the higher hill slopes where the forests once stood. Owarunga went ahead, then came Hugh, and after him the ragged tail of hangers-on. Owarunga had less than basic English. He had achieved a repertoire of kitchen expressions such as: 'Tea is served, Memsahib,' or, 'Coffee is on the veranda, Bwana.' In any case, even the word 'memsahib' was an importation, and like the other foreign words he warped it into his own manner of speaking, so it took an accustomed ear to know he was not talking Swahili or Somali or his own Kikuyu tongue.

Out on their exploration he left behind his kitchen repertoire and he and the white man fell back on their own natures. Owarunga knew that Hugh would want to see things for himself, and he padded swiftly on, pausing to shout at the boys or at times standing aside so the Englishman could take the lead. At one of the pauses Hugh walked ahead and came on something, to him, strangely startling. A huge yellow caterpillar tractor lay abandoned below the lumber track half swallowed by the oncoming bush. It

looked undamaged, though a season or more's growth of
the wild was crawling over it; down on one side and the
upper track rearing off the ground, as if it had died making
a last desperate plunge for the road.

They all stood in a huddle on the damp mossy path above.
A slow drizzle had been filtering down through the trees,
but the clouds were breaking and sun patches made the wet
paintwork of the big machine gleam bright against the darkness of green and grey, of leaf, bark and lichen.

Owarunga had specially wanted him to see the abandoned
giant, he knew that. The little man stood with downcast
eyes, yet nothing could hide his excitement, as though he
were in the presence of a great and profound mystery, of
Death itself. They had passed other derelict and broken-
down machinery – a tiller almost invisible in a matted and
overgrown coffee plantation, a mule plough upside down
with its mould-board removed. And first of all Hugh had
been shown the well with a little pumping plant that no
longer worked. The pump shafts had gone rusty, and that
was a sore point with Owarunga because he had to draw
up water hand over hand with a rope and a milking-bucket.
Quite a deep well too; the timber hatch had been lifted off
and there was no winding gear and nothing to stop the
piccanins from falling in if they played there incautiously.
Owarunga seemed to take it as inevitable that he must pull
one of them, drowned, out of the well some future day.
He pointed down the dark echoing well-shaft and then at
the clump of sniffing little boys and shook his head mildly.
And they all felt grieved at the impending disaster, though
not for long. Hugh Beauchamp shook his head, too, and
wondered which of the audience Owarunga would have to
hoist lifeless from the dark water below.

They had gone on from the well into the fringe of the forest. The inventory Hugh had from the solicitors handling his uncle Jago's will had shown a forest area of two square miles. That might have been a piece of optimism. But whatever it was, there was nothing left of the forest save a few big trees on the inaccessible heights and deep in a ravine falling towards the Rift escarpment. For the rest, only bush remained, thick and wild, and the stumps of the felled trees – podo, cedar, African teak – trees that had grown over the centuries. Owarunga had wanted Hugh to see them too, and had tapped with his stick on each stump they passed.

'There's the devil in him, no doubt,' Hugh thought, recalling Owarunga's solemn officiousness. 'No wonder Mich feels it a duty to fill him with lead.'

Owarunga had next taken him to the cattle-sheds and around the home paddocks. Money had been spent like water at one time on the fences and buildings of Upper Gilgit. Uncle Jago's inventory listed hundreds of cattle in the estate left to Hugh. Yet again, like the trees of the forest-land, they were not to be seen. Or rather, there were a few score lying about contentedly in the overgrown grass at which Owarunga pointed with a disdainful sniff. He was not a cattle-man; in fact he had a certain aloofness about cattle deriving from an aversion to the cattle-owning Masai. But that did not stop him from making grand sweeping gestures towards the lush pasture-lands dotted with gauzy green acacia trees to contrast their emptiness with a time when large herds roamed there. *Sic transit gloria*, this seemed to be his theme, but expressed in mime and some grumblings of Kikuyu. Sure, he was enjoying the rôle of goading the new Bwana against the displaced one whom he had served for eight years past. He wanted Hugh to see how his substance had been squandered. And perhaps in the back of his thoughts was some vague idea that Hugh might take the whiteman's equivalent of a bush-knife and shed his cousin's blood. That would make a day to remember and talk about long into life.

Hugh wasn't that kind of a savage. He was not likely to fall for Owarunga's line, though he was fascinated by the little man. Neither was he letting Mich impress him. Poor old Mich was trying to make his skin creep and had remarked more than a few times on the appalling strain and danger of life at Upper Gilgit Farm. Mich and Evvy were like a pair of blind moles whose burrow had been invaded. There was nothing they more patently craved than to be rid of him. Still, he had inherited the whole estate in Uncle Jago's will and the boot was on the other foot. They were there on sufferance, not he.

Mich's full name was Miles Chudleigh Beauchamp. 'Mich' was a school nickname that had stuck; some of the family used it with a suspicion of contempt, others with friendliness, and Evvy called him Michy with a satisfied affection, as if she had invented it – and him – herself. So he did not mind. From a distance he had the stamp of the Beauchamps – tall and powerful but with a stoop of the shoulders, a good profile, rounded forehead and high-bridge nose. Only coming near you were taken aback by the unexpectedness of his person. He seemed to have got blurred like a clay model of something fine that has been mishandled. It wasn't drink either; Evvy saw to that. Eyes once a crisp hazel had got fogged among heavy flesh that was not so much wrinkled as degenerate. The colour of him, too, was a peculiar coppery-red, perhaps from the hard light of the equatorial highlands, a light which does not tan white men, but seems rather to flay them alive.

From early boyhood his father had been acidly disappointed in him. Mortimer Beauchamp was interested in sport and not much else, and to his mind his son was a total failure. That meant he was totally ungifted in any branch of sport. Mortimer had been known to speak to his cronies about 'that blithering arse, my son.' Only Mich's mother kept faith in him, and it was she who created and nursed the family tradition that the boy was an inventive genius, the equal of Edison or Marconi if only he were given the chance. He had been given a good many chances by different members of the family, especially by bachelor Uncle Jago, and he was always on the point of patenting some sensational invention whose royalties would make a million. Now he was a shade over fifty and the tradition of his invention was like the story of King John's treasure. It was in the Wash and would never be anywhere else.

At the end of World War I he had been a subaltern in the R.A.S.C. and met a pretty little ranker of the Women's Auxiliary. Fanny Dibble considered she had done well marrying a Beauchamp; she preferred to be known afterwards as Everill, and would say to new acquaintances: 'The name is pronounced Bew-shum, you know. A very old family, nobody knows how old, of course. There were Bewshums in the Crusades.' The enthusiasm was short-lived. In time, Evvy developed a slow, passionate and consuming hatred for the Beauchamp family and anything connected with them. Then it was 'Those corny Bo-chumps, take my oath! The nose, the profile, don't you know, ha, ha!'

Mich did not mind at all. He found it exciting to have Evvy tear into the relations, and he would add his own bit against the memory of his father, Mortimer. 'That old bastard,' he rumbled, 'never cared a damn if I were alive or dead. What did he leave me when he died of drink, two thousand in debts!'

The contempt of a parent for the child is seed of a poisonous growth. And in Mich it was utter disaster. He had become a burden on the family, hating them and wheedling them by turns. Each failure sank him deeper. He took refuge behind Evvy – she never admitted he had failed in anything, or could fail. More and more desperately as it wore thinner he paraded the illusion of his great inventions.

Uncle Jago had fixed Selwyn with his first of many jobs in an export business in Nairobi. That was a time when Mich was on the point of patenting a novel idea in food processing, using seaweed and potatoes and some other secret ingredient. But nothing came of it, and Mich and Evvy followed their son to Kenya. World War II caught up with them there, and Mich climbed into uniform again and did a base job in Nairobi for four years, his longest sustained effort. Nobody quite knew what he did, though he went on doing it and could not back out. When it came to an end, Uncle Jago put him on Upper Gilgit and himself returned to live in a comfortable old family house in Bath.

'But for Evvy, the hyenas would have cleaned Mich up,' he said. 'They couldn't stomach her.' Nor could he.

Mich made his greatest mistake, the crowning failure of his life, thinking Upper Gilgit would become his legacy. Uncle Jago's last joke was to leave the estate instead to Hugh, only son of his youngest brother Edward. He had his joke and they (almost) had his estate, as Dryden said of the noble lord. The joke nearly broke Mich and Evvy.

'My inventory talks about a couple of square miles of timber,' Hugh said suddenly after Owarunga had finally padded out, 'what became of the trees?'

Mich had those foggy eyes fixed on him and a half-smile pulling at his mouth, but slowly his face was going purple.

'Trees,' he managed to say at last. 'Trees? What trees?'

'Trees from the stumps up on the heights. Miles and miles of stumps.'

'Stumps . . . ah . . . Bush clearance.'

'Not bush, Miles. I'm talking about those whacking great stumps, four or five feet across, some of them. Was the timber cut before your time?'

'Ha, ha, ha! I see what you mean.'

'Not in my time. Five feet across – do you hear that, Ev?'

Evvy went on re-arranging a pot of snake-lilies and put a cloth straight on a glass table. She turned her sharp face, terribly pale but for the streak of lipstick and a few big dark freckles that the tropical light had turned into permanent stains on her skin.

'Did I hear! So much timber, and it's funny I never had enough firewood for the kitchen stove.'

'Don't get excited, Hugh,' Mich said hoarsely.

'I am curious.'

'So am I, ha, ha! To know where the lawyers got that stuff about two square miles of timber. Jago was a doddering old fool the last eight years of his life but I never rated him a bare-faced liar.'

'I knew Uncle Jago and saw him often. I think you are

wrong.'

The couple had got over the first tension. They had dreaded this moment but now they were braced and ready to meet their attacker. They expected him to go on and demand an account of every log and every cow and coffee tree on the farm. They had gone by degrees over the years, through bad management or sometimes through unconsidered, even panicky effort to raise money, mainly for Selwyn. Selwyn always needed money. They crept and wrung their hands and went in agony for him. If only Jago had left them the estate things might have been smoothed out; no questions, no demands. They had counted blindly on that and in the end here was the true owner, Hugh Beauchamp, to call for an account.

'Well?' Mich challenged.

'Well, I shall be back in Nairobi tomorrow. I may possibly see you before I leave for England, but for two weeks I'm doing a sort of safari southwards into Tanganyika.'

'You're not staying!' Evvy said blankly.

'Tonight only. I shall have to leave very early, if you don't mind, to catch the party.'

'You don't mean to make your home in Africa?'

'No, Miles.'

'Smarter than I gave you credit for.'

'Thanks.'

'You are a deep fellow, Hugh, and that's not a family failing.'

'I've heard a lot from the family about you.'

'Me!'

'Your talent for inventions.' Mich's mouth fell open. 'Oh yes, my father used to say you invented a little gadget when you married that nudged you and made you turn over if you snored.

'Ha, ha, ha!' Mich roared. 'I never snore!'

But his face had darkened with blood. They were laughing at him, the pestilential family. He would like to take them one by one and throttle the breath out of them. He thought his cousin was baiting him. But Hugh was trying to work out in his mind what to do with Upper Gilgit Farm – whether to leave Miles on it and see him go bankrupt or to sell it as it stood and grant his cousin interest for life on the capital. Either way he would earn the undying hatred of the couple, if he hadn't done so already. But he had the money, more than enough for himself, and after all Miles was his nearest relative. Uncle Jago had gone too far with the kind of wicked cynicism that ran in the family and he could see to it that his cousin was not wrecked by the old man's quirk.

'What's going to become of us, of me and Evvy and Selwyn? I mean, where do we come in?' Mich started; he had come down to wheedling and let the tatters of his personal dignity go to the devil.

'Why Selwyn? He seems to do very well for himself.'

'Selwyn is our son, our only son. We have to think of him.'

'Oh naturally. Miles, you don't have to worry. Ours may be a queer family, but after all you are my nearest relations, apart from Mother. Why, if I got myself eaten by a lion on this Tanganyika safari you come in as my next of kin.'

It was a poor jest but could not have had a poorer reception. Mich gaped across at him, and Evvy sat rigid staring down at her hands inert in her lap. Suddenly she looked up, her face wrenched with a cold bitter passion.

'No, thanks you, Mr Hugh Bo-chump! We have had enough of being the next of kin. Always the next and the next but never belonging. You can keep your kin and your family of Bo-chumps. What have we ever got out of them, I ask you that? Sweet Fanny Adams! . . . All right, let me say what I have to say, let me tell you the facts and you can be as mean as your uncle Jago Bo-chump – beg pardon, Bew-shum. That old scoundrel, never did a hand's turn in his life and stinking with money he didn't deserve. And here Michy was, working himself to the bone, throwing away his valuable time and talents, for what? All for that old hyena. And in the end did he get left anything? Not a watch or a ring, not a brass farthing. Everybody in the damn family got his slice. You got your cool hundred thousand quid, Mr Hugh Bew-shum, and you already had even more from your father. Uncle Edward – he knew how to look after the main chance. But what did my husband get? Yes, you can look at me like that. What a family! And you talk about next of kin. No, thanks.'

She clutched at her neck, almost choking, and tears ran down her pale marked cheeks. Mich had gone to her in great agitation and laid his big hands on her quivering shoulders.

'My dear Evvy. Please, Evvy, please!'

Then he looked up at his cousin with a curious blind pride. 'Something in what she says.'

'Indeed there is.'

'Always comes straight from the shoulder with Evvy. No beating about the bush.'

So deep were his love and trust that he could admire her even then. He could never see the soul of Evvy, the barrenness and hate that bit like a corrosion into all that her life touched. He brought her a glass of water and the three of them sat uncomfortably in the walled-in room trying to talk neutrally while the wind boomed outside and unknown things slithered down the thatch roof.

'Hear it?' Mich said. 'Wonderful thing about Africa. A huge, high-powered machine running in low gear. Been here long enough and I should know. A machine powered by the sun, sparked by the genius of the whiteman. Off the production lines roll the endless trains of wealth. Takes a lot of learning but the whole thing's perfect. Everything perfect, timed to a second. Waiting for the next change of gear.'

Hugh thought he was joking. 'You mean the way the farms are run? And the Emergency?'

'The Emergency is another thing,' he smiled, holding what looked like a cigarette pack partly concealed in his hand. 'Take a look at this.' There was a sudden movement and the muzzle of a miniature automatic popped out close to Hugh's face. It gave him a start he could not conceal.

'Ha ha! That took you off guard. A precision gun with a little trick to it – a thing I invented myself. The Emergency took some people off guard. But I saw it coming. I warned them. The machine has its rhythm and you must understand and manage it.'

Hugh took and examined the trick gun. It was a cheap Japanese make. He handed it back without saying anything and let his cousin go on talking.

'People sometimes ask what I did in the war and all that, you know. Didn't I take a back seat, etcetera. You remember the Battle of Britain?'

'I was at school at the time.'

'Yes, I keep forgetting your age. Well, I was on secret

research. I sent in to the Air Ministry my design for an aero-carburettor. It was not startling, but just had that difference. Gave the Spitfire and Hurricane pilots an extra quarter of an hour in the air. Goering had everything calculated – except those extra fifteen minutes. You see what I mean? We won the battle.'

Evvy was watching him through lowered lids and her head on one side like a mother watching her infant playing. He was in his element. Going over to the desk he took from a drawer a complicated casting in light metal. He handled it with an air of its tremendous value and delicacy, allowed Hugh to hold it for a moment before slipping it back, smiling, into the desk. It was a part of a standard aviation engine.

'Then I was sent to Washington to keep the Americans up to the level in technique. I had some tussles with them until I found the line to follow. Every new idea I wanted them to take up I had to make out they had invented themselves. It always worked. Even the atom bomb. They wouldn't use it unless they thought it was their big hunch.' He laughed at the notion of deceiving the vainglorious Americans.

'But here's something,' he went on. 'Take a look at this little gadget.'

He selected from a glass-cabinet of knick-knacks a flat, metal cigarette-lighter. 'It has a history you may not believe. We had been getting reports that the Nazis were working on quick extermination methods in the concentration camps by injection. They were using petrol, carbon-tetrachloride, even air bubbles, and timing the efficiency. Another line of research was to find a substance that killed without leaving a trace. I solved both problems and combined them in this lighter. Don't get too near, Hugh.'

He flicked up the spring top, producing a flame. Simultaneously a fine needle like a sting darted out with a tiny jet of fluid. 'That of course is just water. Not the real stuff. When Rommel was holding up our advance in France we dropped a top agent near his H.Q. He was in German uniform and armed with nothing but one of my lighters. Rommel died, you understand. I always felt bad about it. After all he was a fine soldier. The Jerrys claimed they assassinated Rommel themselves – couldn't stand the idea the enemy outclassed them.'

He was tuned up. From the broiling Nissen hut in Nairobi where he had had his knees under a desk he had dreamed his high adventures. He was a great killer who succeeded always and came out from each exploit honourably unscathed. Hugh wanted somehow to bring the epic to an end. Miles was feeling things badly and the tension had swung his mind out on this tangent. He needed careful handling and the question of the estate was going to be complicated. Things would have to be managed indirectly, through the executors of Uncle Jago's will, so that Miles and Evvy were provided with a reasonable income in an official and impersonal arrangement. It would save them from bankruptcy and also keep them at arm's length. He did not want his cousin to come wheedling to him for capital.

'What are you thinking?' Mich turned on him suspiciously.

'I was listening to you.'

'Thinking deep, Hugh.'

'I'm off to bed,' Everill said.

'Bed-time already, dear! You will excuse us, Hugh, we country folk keep early hours. See you in the morning,

Huge. Hope you'll be comfortable and safe.'

'Thanks, I'm sure I shall. I'll have to be off in the morning at five.'

'Five!' he glanced at Evvy and felt the chill of a stony look in her set grey eyes. 'Oh well, then if I don't see you – good hunting.'

Everill had brewed coffee on a spirit-lamp to save her from calling in the suspected Owarunga, and the three of them sipped their cups in a racking silence. Evvy went out with a curt good night, followed by Mich. Hugh turned on the radio and a dance came on dreamily while he tried to think of this strange encounter with his cousin. He was deeply drowsy – the great altitude and the undeniable strain of the day at Upper Gilgit. He took his lamp and groped off to bed.

After a few minutes they heard his heavy breathing. They found he had not undressed but fallen on the divan in his clothes and his face was half buried in the pillow. A young man of good physique and high health, his cheek-bones a sun-tinged pink and the white smooth skin going away into thick black hair at the temples and forehead.

'Now,' Everill said.

'It's too risky.'

'Nonsense – he won't wake with an elephant in the house. I put five tablets in his coffee.'

'It's not that. He looks, kind of, too healthy to die a natural death.'

'That will all go. He won't look so healthy. Make the injection inside the nose and it will never be seen.'

Mich's scorched-red face had blenched and the fading colour left him a bluish grey, startling to Everill.

'Better to hit him with a panga and fix the blame on

Owarunga,' he said.

'Who'll hit him?'

Mich merely shuddered and looked at her appealingly. She was so inexorable.

'No,' she went on, 'your first idea is better. The injection will be over in a moment and leave no trace.'

'My idea!'

'You perfected it.'

'Ah!'

'Don't waste time. You have the hypodermic?'

'Yes, I brought it, but wait a minute. . . .'

'What's the matter?'

'Evvy, it's too dangerous.'

'Listen, he must never wake up or we are ruined. Yes, you know that. He is going to turn us out. He will sue you in the courts for those trees and the cattle and everything. Think I don't know his type? Playing smooth and friendly but the minute he leaves he will set the lawyers on to us. In a day he knows everything; didn't he spy out the farm while we were asleep? Yes, you know it. But if anything happens to him we are next of kin. You heard him say that.'

'He said something of the kind. But he was lying, lying! I'm certain of it.'

'No, listen to me. It's true. I know the Beauchamp family backwards. Hugh hasn't had time to make a new will. You would certainly come into Jago's estate, if not more. We could die feeling that Selwyn will be provided for.'

'Ah, maybe that is all so. But I can't – I can't do it.'

'Give me the hypodermic.'

'No. No, Evvy. Oh Christ.'

'What's come over you now?'

'It's no good. I never managed to get the right chemical.

123

I never managed it – do you hear! There's nothing in that syringe, nothing that would kill a baby. Only a little water and iodine.'

'Of course I knew you were still experimenting and you will get the formula yet. So meanwhile I brought some petrol.'

'Petrol! I can't do it. Petrol isn't safe. They would find out. For certain.'

'Give me the syringe.'

'Evvy, we have got to think of something else.'

'Quick now – there's no time to waste.'

'I tell you I can't, I can't, I can't!'

'You can. Do you hear me? You can.'

'No – no-o-o.' He was gasping for breath and his big hands clasped together, trembling.

'Ah! You are a fine one, you are. There's only one thing you have to do. So simple, just a little guts and you can put paid to the man who has robbed you of your heritage, you and me and Selwyn. You can pay back the whole score. Didn't they all hate you and cheat you and despise you for forty years?'

'I know . . .'

'You are twice the man they are. Now is the time to prove it.'

'Oh Evvy, you don't know what you are saying.'

He sat in a grass chair and slumped forward helplessly. There seemed to be nothing left in him. He could not move, he could not look at her. At last he stretched out and took her hand, but she jerked away.

'None of that snivelling. Are you going on with this or not? Just tell me if you mean to ruin the lot of us?'

'I can't. It won't work. Nothing works.'

She knew so well that cry of desperation. Since their marriage more and more urgently she had been hearing it and never once had she failed him when he made it. Always her faith had raised him and shaken him out and knitted together his tottering confidence. So often that she had taken over from his mother and become the mainstay of his life, nurse of his illusions she sometimes half believed in herself.

He wanted her to protect him again, but she drew away.

'I've had enough of your slobbering, I have,' she said tight-lipped with fury. 'Nothing works – that's the truest thing you ever said. At least, nothing you ever touched. Don't think you ever fooled me, but now it comes to this, you can't even fool yourself . . .'

'Evvy,' he cried out, 'Evvy, stop!'

'Oh yes, it's time you knew what a big busted windbag you are. Everything you say is a lie because you are a coward. You're scared. You're scared of the truth and the truth is you are a miserable bloody failure and you can't hide it any more in all your silly lies.'

He had stood up and once more cried out to her wildly: 'Evvy, Evvy! Stop!'

'Don't come near me, I'm sick of you. D'you think your cousin Hugh Beauchamp believed a thing you said tonight? Ha ha ha! You bet he did! Look at him, smiling even in his sleep, laughing at you. Yes, look at him – look . . .'

He had caught her; his hands were big and damp and still trembling. But he had caught her to stop the words that were annihilating him, sweeping him into nothingness. He covered her mouth and nose. He could not let go. If only she would stop, stop. It wasn't her – Evvy hadn't said things like that. She couldn't.

Her hands relaxed and she slipped to the floor. He picked

her up and put her on the chair. Now there was blood on her mouth and a queer angle about the set of her neck. She was dead.

Mich knelt in front of her and touched her open eye. He had killed her. He knew it but the knowledge was not whole nor complete; it was disconnected from him. He was somebody else who had a dead body in the chair. What had happened? He did not remember and he did not try to sort it out because he was not concerned; somebody else was. He found himself taking her up and carrying her outside to the well. The well was dark and deep and secret. He tied Owarunga's rope carefully under her arms and lowered her gently, hand over hand into the well.

Mich was asleep when Hugh left and he woke about sunrise with a feeling of excitement. He was missing Evvy a lot. He knew where she was and it was time she came up. He had always meant to invent and install a scientific winch on the well, even since the pump-engine caved in.

The mornings were cold before sunrise and he pulled on a pair of thick corduroys and a duffle-coat and went out. Nobody around. It would take only a jiffy to help her out, but no one must see. It would be a secret between them.

'Time to come up,' he whispered down the black, oozing well-shaft and the echoes made a faint rustling sound. Then something touched him on the shoulder, and in the fright it gave him he nearly lost his balance.

'Tea is served for Bwana,' Owarunga was saying almost in his ear.

He wanted to bawl at the little black man. But quite suddenly he changed his mind. Turning his face cunningly he said to the servant: 'And don't forget the Memsahib. Make another pot, I will have my tea together with her.'

Owarunga was not being taken in. He stepped forward and peered boldly down the well. Then he rose to a new accomplishment in his kitchen English: 'Nottee for'd Memsabu.'

Going back to the kitchen Owarunga plucked a leaf as he passed a bush and bit into it, fresh and acid. The white people were mad in any case, he thought. He could have understood the Bwana Hugh being knocked out and thrown down the well. But Hugh had tipped him a whole crackling pound note and gone off in his car while the morning star still shone, and down in the black water instead was the Memsahib. No use thinking about these things. Still, he wasn't making a second pot of tea for her, and that was flat.

Franz fumbled a little tying the reins of his horse to the post under the great cypress tree and stood then with both hands on the saddle. He gazed up at his home. Close around him was the hot scented shade. A small stain of shade very dark as if the great and whispering height of the tree made up in sheer density against the sun what it lacked in the leafage of more generous trees. His legs were stiff, unused to riding, and there was a sharp edge of weariness, not unpleasant, in his back. Franz de la Rey liked the steaming smell of the horse and the creaking of stirrup leathers in the saddle. They called up a sentimental picture he cherished to balance his present smallness against a more heroic past. His forebears were pioneers, men of the smooth-bore rifle, the covered trek-wagon and laager; men welded in the saddle, welded and tempered in fire; conquerors. As he looked across the horse's rump at his home the thoughts rose and burst faintly like bubbles behind his eyes leaving his mind empty, a blank, and only a heavy mood stayed to darken his homely open face.

He was more used to the driving-seat and the simple plastic controls of his maroon and biscuit-coloured Studebaker. The car fatigued him stealthily with insidious comfort. But the hard old saddle of his father took punishment out of him for his softness. The living, uncompromising curve of the horse's bulk shaped out against his untrained legs, straining joints, chafing up skin. Where he had been he could not go in a car. He had ridden because he had no other way of getting there and it had been no pleasure ride; no heroics, no gold-splashed dreams of his ancestors long ago. The horse was blown and foam-flecked, but it had lapsed out of his consciousness and he did not think to loosen the girth or rub down the saddle marks. He was young, ruddy-skinned and had brown curly hair with a shine in it under the sun and his eyes now were full of trouble, of anger and fear, a lost look, disillusioned, resentful.

Franz saw his dog, a tan setter beautiful in every point, get up from the stoep and come into the hot sun. Lazily it stretched and yawned and its clean pink tongue curved upwards as if on a spring. The setter was a dignified dog, almost insolent. It made no show of being too excited over Franz's comings and goings and now came trotting down the path in the dust swinging the long feather of its tail like a stately fan. Franz pushed aside the fine head of the dog and it took the snub calmly, going on to have a familiar sniff at the horse's nose. Satisfied, it turned to follow its master back to the house. But half-way to the homestead the setter stopped in the path. An unusual manner about the man made him stop, the way he walked, quick and jerky. A hint of danger in a man walking like that with turmoil enough inside him to be picked up by the alert senses of the hunting dog.

Three new concrete steps took Franz up to the new stoep of painted woodwork, glass screens and a floor of green plastic tiles. Green for coolness! How could a colour make any cooler the shimmering white-heat of January noon in the thornveld? She thought it could. Aletta thought so and she had modern ideas. Aletta did everything about the house; she had changed everything until there remained no recognisable feature of the old home of his father and grandfather

E

and great-grandfather. The poky little voorkamer had gone, heart of the boer-house with its dung-smeared clay floors, and with it the dark, small sitting-room. The sitting-room had always spoken to him of the mystery, the suppressed and unspoken things of his family. He remembered with awe the four black chairs and black table and a bible-desk inlaid with a star in ivory; the Brown Bess musket and an ox-horn powder-flask hung above the fireplace that had never been lit to his knowledge, just as the room had never been used, except once for his mother's funeral. The key-hole of the room used to moan softly with the draught, though mostly it was silent, charged with its musky animal smell, with secrecy and gloom. He had been excited and also disturbed far down in his feelings when Aletta had partitions knocked down, big windows, glass doors punched into the old thick outer walls, plaster and paint slapped over the shale and basalt stonework. And colours, colours to heighten her happiness, to make illusions of coolness or joy or love. While she had done these things he had worshipped her, followed her in everything with a primal ache in his heart of terrible possession. With her near, his old feeling of awe for the family past sank away to nothing.

This girl was his, his, in all her convolutions and inner strangeness solely his possession. But not always. She could stand apart from him, retreat into an exclusive self. He dreaded his own future then, the wonder of love, the agony of it was too overwhelming to last. Her separateness and her potency to move subtly out of his range held over his head a curious dismay filling him with inadequacy and powerlessness.

He came into the softly furnished lounge she had created out of the hard and uncompromising house of his fathers.

And there she was. His heart stopped as she uncurled from a corner of the settee and stood to greet him. At first he saw the involuntary little dent of happiness in her smile that made him reel and his limbs grow weak. Then she must have caught the bitterness in his face and her eyes went dark and big as she came across the Persian carpet to him. Her eyes then looked to him deep, all pupil, containing in a single moment all his soul clung to, and yet able to shut him out as if by the mere closing of her lids.

'O Franz,' she said. That was all. And she put her hands on his shoulders and he smelt her breath sweet like ripe quinces, sweet, drugging. He backed a step. A moment later he had done something he did not know was in his power. He took her hands off him and let them drop and he brushed past her, going out at the glass door that led to the cool back of the house. He knew she would be watching him, stunned, and the dog would be standing in the doorway to the green-paved stoep watching him too.

How deliriously mad he had been in his surrender, a sub-mission so profound that he could not take a breath, or speak to a stranger without her essence rising in him with a kind of bubbling confusion. People had laughed at him and he laughed with them because that was the limitless measure of his happiness. Now he was beginning to see things as though he had been blind and the light had struck a whip-lash through his eyeballs. That green stoep – he had fancied in his daze that her work had been like the building of Solomon's chariot, 'the midst thereof being paved with love'. But it was a green plastic paving to create the silly illusion of coolness after she had cut down the old gum and juniper trees to open a view to the snow-topped mountains a hun-dred miles away. She had spared the single great cypress because he had told her his father's favourite dog was buried under it. And she loved dogs. She also loved his father and her curious assurance had won the old man to her side.

Franz went into the bedroom. He did not want her to come in and he stood listening for her steps while his heart in its darkness boomed at his throat. He was afraid because he had gone so far that he could not turn back. Not if he wished. The thing was clear and he had no choice but to go on the way he had started.

Four years after his mother's death his father had a heart attack and only by a miracle, so the doctors said, he had recovered. Christiaan de la Rey was one of the wealthiest farmers in the district and he could afford easily to follow the doctor's orders to retire and live at the sea-coast. He bought himself a house at Doonside Beach and there he lived a comfortable jovial sort of life with a housekeeper and three servants and any of the de la Rey relations, no matter how distant, who cared to accept Oom Christiaan's open hospitality. And many of them did. Christiaan was popular with the relatives and the neighbours and holiday-makers and especially with children. They thought the stout mahogany-faced old man with surprisingly blue eyes and a little white goatee beard was some kind of a friendly spirit whose purpose in life was to tell marvellously funny stories and produce surprises out of his baggy pockets. Christiaan turned over the running of his farms with four thousand sheep and a large beef herd to his only son – Franz. The same year Franz and Aletta were married. Franz had kept trusted headmen on the farms and mostly he left them to look after the sheep and cattle. Aletta had spent the time they were home rebuilding and redecorating the main farmstead, but that could not remain the driving purpose of her life. Her creative centre was somewhere else, and soon she would grow restless, sad. Franz knew her moods to a hair and so it became a joke with them to look at one another and say almost in one breath: 'Well – shall we go?' They went to the Victoria Falls and to the National Park. They took a trip up the coast to Portuguese East Africa and gambled in the casinos, not heavily, because they were beginners. They drove a thousand miles to Cape Town to watch a Rugby test match against the British Lions team. Each trip had been to Franz like a honeymoon. Their real honeymoon had misfired; they had gone to Madagascar in a French ship and Aletta got a touch of fever in Tananarive. Still, they had made up for it. In between their longer expeditions they thought nothing of week-ends in the city or a flying visit to have Sunday dinner with old Christiaan. The farms paid. The cattle bred and thrived and had to be sold to keep down their numbers. The wool clip paid handsomely. Making money was easy as falling in a dam.

Then Christiaan suggested a check-up and Franz found one flock of over a thousand sheep no less than six hundred short. Six hundred! More than half gone. He was so staggered he felt he had been punched on the jaw. 'Where are they? Where are they?' he kept saying. He sat on an ant-heap under the blazing sun and in his bewilderment and frustration he did not notice his eyes fill with tears.

'The jackals took many, my basie. Others died of blue-tongue, gall-sickness,' a headman said.

'Gall-sickness to hell!' he bawled, springing up. His face had turned livid. 'You lost them! You stole them, and you have the nerve to talk about gall. God damn you! Where are they?'

The headman lowered his eyes, dark, black slits, dark glinting holes, black with malice.

'My basie cannot say I took them. What have I done with them then?'

'Well, you know. You know where they went.'

'I told my basie.'

'It's a lie, curse you, filthy thing!'

There were losses in the other flocks, but not so heavy. All told, less than a thousand he could not account for. He was unable to hide it for one minute from Aletta. She came to meet him as he climbed out of the Studebaker.

'Franzie,' she said gravely. 'Something is wrong.'

The setting sun, he remembered, shone on her thick light hair but her eyes remained cool and deep like the darkness of a valley after sunset. And after he had faltered it out she said: 'But, my treasure, we still have three thousand.'

'How am I going to tell Father?'

'Tell him of course how bad the sickness and the jackals are.'

'No. He will not believe it. He couldn't. I myself don't believe it. No. He would have another heart attack.'

'Ah heaven! Franzie – that's true.'

'I have to find those sheep.'

'But where?'

'I have to find them.'

They had gone up to the house together and he had gripped her hand like a little boy, helpless, wanting to be consoled, wanting to cry.

In the night he had sat up suddenly in bed. The moon was in the window-panes and the sky like milk. Aletta woke with a little cry seeing him rigid, staring at the window. The setter came in at the bedroom door and flopped on the carpet to scratch.

'Somebody is outside,' Franz whispered.

She put her arms round him, alarmed. 'But there's Rooi; he is not barking. He would bark if there was somebody.'

The dog went on scratching, tapping its hock on the floor with a steady, muffled knock, knock, knock.

'There – it's only Rooi scratching. But what made you think there was someone? My darling, you were dreaming.'

'Yes, I must have been dreaming. I – I was sure, somehow, it was Dismata the witch-doctor.'

He turned to her with a face made much paler in the dimness of the night and his pupils looked dilated, enormous.

'But does not Dismata live far away down in the Bushman Ravine. He would surely never come here. At night.'

'No.'

'Kiss me and go to sleep.'

Still he sat up, staring past her. 'I was thinking of going to see him, to find my sheep. Then I suddenly thought he was outside. Do you think he knew? There's nothing they don't smell out, and I have heard Dismata has often found lost stock for the farmers.'

'Ah,' she whispered with an instinctive shudder. 'Franz, don't think of going to Dismata. Such things come of it. Promise me, Franzie. Those witch-doctors are evil to us, evil. He could do nothing but lead your feet on an evil path.'

'I don't care, if he finds my sheep.'

'And if he does not?'

'He will point to the thief.'

'Franzie, Franzie, you scare me so. Promise me not to think of it.'

He stretched on his back and pulled the sheet up to his

chin. The night was too hot for a blanket. Then his eyes closed and the moon made his face gaunt, bony, bloodless. She thought with a sudden horror of how he would look if she had to lay him out, dead.

Franz afterwards had a recollection before falling asleep again of her fingers softly touching his face, round the curve of his cheeks and along his lips, softly in the near-dark. His heart had squeezed with a strange tenderness. He did not know what she had seen as he lay there with closed eyes.

Am I going to lose her now? he thought, standing in the bedroom and listening for her. There was no sound. He went across and opened a drawer of her dressing-table and took out a garment from among her underclothes, a thing of translucent machine fibre, machine-made lace, machine-patterned – modern, as he thought of it. She was a modern girl and had worked in Johannesburg. He had met her on a holiday at Doonside Beach where his father lived and her town smartness and shine had appealed to his own restlessness, his discontent. But now for the first time he was thrown back on himself; he felt her sympathy and love were not there beyond question for him to lean on. Angrily he stuffed the garment in his pocket, seeing himself fragmented in the three angled mirrors. Deeper in the glass he caught sight of Aletta standing at the door.

'Franz, what have you taken – what do you need that for?'

He stood with his back to her, shoulders hunching. When he turned, his face was deeply flushed and the veins stood out on his neck and temples. She was in the door, quite still and tense with the big dog Rooi at her side and her fingers twined in his silky coat, the crimson of her varnished nails like blood-drops against the iron-red of him. Franz took the garment from his pocket and it unfolded in his outstretched hand.

'That is what I took,' he jerked out with a bitter twist to his mouth.

'But what for, why?'

'You would not understand.'

'No, it's true, I do not understand. You are so strange, Franz.'

They stared across a great distance, over a terrifying depth in this first crisis of their life together. He glanced from her to the dog and back.

'Franz,' she said. 'You have been to Dismata.'

He nodded.

'And it was he who told you to take my bra?'

'He needed certain things.'

She understood, but not as he thought. In the hidden core of her heart was an awareness that she was facing not Dismata the witch-doctor nor Franz's shock and his will to recover the lost sheep. Her instinct went at once to the centre and saw the man in him rising against her – not even against her, but against absorption, domination by her sex. Against love. It took a great heart to endure love and a great spirit to be free. Against the fear of the darkening of his life Franz was groping not into light but into a hell, back into the nightmare of her people, the terror that crept in the small hours of the night when life was weakest and the soul grew small on its lonely flight. She recognised the nightmare; as a woman she knew better than Franz ever could. She knew the awful attraction of it like a dreamer drawn nearer and nearer the brink of a bottomless dream-fall. She had to go softly with him not to wake him violently.

Aletta ordered the dog out in a low voice and it went re-

luctantly, hanging its head and turning up its eyes at her.
Then she closed the door and sat on the bed.

'Franz, you rode all that way. Are you not tired?'

'Tired? No.'

'And hungry?'

'Well——'

'I have never seen Dismata, but of course everyone talks
about him. Is he awful?'

'You can say that again,' he slanged, feeling easier. He
was surprised at her, taking this so calmly, smiling.

'He does strange things, they say.'

'That's just what is so – so queer. He did nothing. Only
sat there looking, looking at me like a devil. Hai! but strange
things happened.'

She was silent, round-eyed, waiting for him to go on. He
knew as surely as anyone could know without putting it
into words that he was being mastered. His resoluteness, his
independence, were being sapped away. But it was so much
more delightful to hold her interest. He drew up the dress-
ing-stool and sat astride it to tell her, and he could always
tell a story better with his slim pliant body relaxed and
hands free for the full play of gesture.

'Ai Hemel!' He shook his head incredulously. 'But you
should have been there. You will never believe it.'

He told her about the witch-doctor. He had been terribly
impressed, appalled, and now it came rolling out and he
almost lost himself in the telling. Dismata used the talking
and whistling spirits. Franz had come into his hut and
crouched in the semi-dark until he saw the face of the
medicine-man solid black, heavy, shining like polished
stone. Then voices shrieked in the soot-blackened roof of
the hut and the hair rose on Franz's neck. Behind him an

old, wicked voice said with a laugh: 'You have lost your sheep!' He turned and found nobody there. So it had gone on. The 'voices' knew exactly why he had come. They chattered among themselves, jeered. Sometimes he picked out clear words, at others only a shrill yell. He was wildly confused by it and unnerved, and he found it difficult to tell her all he had heard, what Dismata had said and what came from the spirits. Difficult – because they had talked about her, about Aletta, not plainly but in a way he grasped quite well. They spoke about a 'lioness with a yellow mane and red claws.' That was her, and he glanced uneasily again at her soft hands and varnished nails. His substance was being wasted away, they had jibed. And they meant, by her.

He skipped that bit of the story and went back to Dismata. The medicine-man had dropped a single stick on the fire which flared like a torch. By its light he seemed to shrink. He was no more a heavy menacing demon, but small, withered. He was naked to the waist and wore a girdle of monkey tails. In ordinary bad guttural Afrikaans he had told Franz he would see the trail of his sheep, but he must bring four things to guide the *totolo*, the whistling spirits.

'Four things,' Franz repeated.

'Haai, Franz,' she whispered, entering in the awe and mystery of his experience. 'They know so much, surely these spirits do not need to be guided. O surely, surely it is better to keep clear of them.'

'So you do believe there are the spirits?'

'I don't know what to believe, only I feel, I still feel it is a path of evil that Dismata will find. Not the trail of your sheep, Franz, but a path of terrible evil. We should never sink down to that, our people. If we sink down to witchcraft in some way a fearful punishment will surely fall on us.'

'Ag! But that is nothing else than superstition. What sort of punishment?'

'That is in God's will, but I think the same that has fallen on the Kafirs. They are in darkness, a thousand years behind us, because they are sunk in witchcraft. They have powers, oh, I know, but turned back into darkness. It stops them from thinking as we do. Franz, let Dismata be a warning to you.'

'You haven't been long enough in the countryside and you don't understand, Aletta. The farmers often go to Dismata, and where's the punishment?'

'Franz, I love you and I am only saying what comes from my heart.'

'Ja, ja.' He stood up impatiently and went to stare out of the window. A gay-striped canvas awning threw a square of shade and beyond it was the white quivering heat and the shrill of cicadas coming up sharp as if a part with the vibration of the sun itself. He was sorry now he had told her, and he waited tensely for her to ask about the four things Dismata wanted. How would he get over that difficulty? Rather than face up to it he thought of dropping the scheme altogether. He was afraid of Dismata, in a way; the medicine-man had found a chink in his soul, a feeling of paralysis that halted his will. Aletta had warned him and the warning went closer than she could suspect. He found it uncanny that she said nothing now, and left him to struggle with himself. The setter dog came in sight trotting through Aletta's parched little north garden among lines of marigolds and zinnias. He turned from the window.

'What if I don't go back to Dismata? I can make another plan, and I need not pay him.'

'Did he ask for payment?'

'An ox to make the spirits talk.'

She knew he must have agreed to the payment, but still she said nothing, running a ribbon slowly through her fingers. It was torture to him.

'I did not tell you what that witch-doctor wanted, and you don't ask,' he said sharply. 'Why are you putting on this act? Is it to shame me out of something you are scared about, or don't you want to know?'

'One of the things I know already – my underclothes. How insulting, Franz, that he makes such conditions. What the others are I don't like to guess.'

'So little you know, and you say it in a way to put me in the wrong.'

'I just felt hurt that you could take that man something so personal as my bra.'

Franz was in a position where he knew explanations could only make matters worse. But there was still more to come, and he persisted doggedly.

'You understand, that Kafir did not ask for this or that – how can he know what a white woman wears? He just said bring something of yours, I mean something you wear – against your skin.' His face had darkened.

'Why something of mine? – I have not lost the sheep.'

'Mine too, don't worry. A part from my car and a part from a plough.'

'Weird . . . what ideas! And what else?'

He still kept her fixed with that dark stubborn look. 'Weird, yes. The other thing he wants is the fat from my dog's body.'

She caught her breath and a silence thickened between them. At last he said: 'That is the other thing you wanted to know.'

'How awful.' She ignored his tone. 'The fat from poor Rooi's body. He tells you to kill Rooi.'

'Blood always comes into these things. I believe it once used to be human blood,' he added, with a harsh laugh.

'How can you make a joke when you were ready to kill Rooi – for witchcraft?'

'Who says I would kill him? I could take some sheep's fat.'

'And cheat the spirits?'

'Ag, this kind of talk makes me sick!' He flung open the door and stamped out. Once he had started he rushed on and in a moment was striding down the path he had walked up so full of trouble and foreboding a while back. The stable-boy had taken his horse from under the cypress and there was only the enormous dark-green pinnacle of the tree rearing up from the density of its shade. He stopped in the shade, smelling the resinous scent that oozed subtly from the presence of the tree like myrrh. It reminded him of his childhood and the strong all-embracing being of his father. The tree was all he had left to cling to that sky-clear past. She had cut the others down, cut everything from under his feet. She had even won over his father, and he could see how the old man's face came to life in Aletta's presence. It had been a shock to him to find his father looking at her unawares, as a young man looks at a girl with a quiet speechless satisfaction. Now the tree reminded him of his father, not the funny old idler uprooted and cast adrift on the ocean shore, but the Boer with his flat felt hat down tight on his brow, astride his black horse with a fine plaited whip trailing behind him and his dog following, a liver-and-white pointer. The dog lay buried under a smooth square flagstone at the foot of the cypress. That was why Aletta had spared the tree.

Franz sat on the stone, his eyes narrowed and the vision turned inwards on his memories, trying not to lose the picture of his father as he had been in all his strength. Enough for the whole family; not that his mother lacked a kind of tenacious strength, but she was dazzled, withered by the constant heat of Christiaan's energy, like a small old flower. There was no doubt he would have to account for the sheep to Christiaan. If he did not find them. The one really difficult term Dismata had made was the stipulation for the fat of his dog. He was sure, from their uncanny insight, that the medicine-man and his *totolos* would trace the sheep. He was quite sure. And it would be a triumph his father would appreciate when he told how he had done it. If Rooi had to die, he could be buried there under the same stone at the foot of the tree. He was not going to be sentimental about that. Except for Aletta. He had known right from the first moment what this would mean. It was the acid test of himself, of his whole character, his self-possession and his will.

He had not eaten and it seemed hours since his return. The shadow was moving away and the sun came burning on him. He must go through the repugnant business with Rooi, though it would be better if he were alone and could get Aletta away on a visit. Strange how his thoughts separated them now – him and her. Two beings, opposite poles, individual, and between them an unsuspected, unmeasured gulf. Never since they were married had he thought of either going anywhere without the other. Now he wanted her out of the way.

When he stood up at last he was surprised to see a woman and a small boy waiting some way off, patiently squatting in the dust. They were black and both were thin and tired, dressed in a few shapeless and filthy tatters.

'Yes?' he demanded. 'What is it?'

'My basie, I have come for the ox.'

'The ox. . . . I don't know what you are talking about.'

'For Dismata, my basie.'

'What! He has not found my sheep.'

'The spirits talked, the ox is his . . .'

'Verdom!' Franz swore.

'He said the basie was afraid, he said you would not come again because you did not have enough liver. Thus he sent me after you to fetch his ox. I am his woman.'

'Lord God!' Franz murmured in an agony to himself. And he shouted to the hag: 'Go back. You can tell him I am coming again. You can tell him that – you understand!'

He strode up to the house, and from the green-paved stoep he could see Aletta moving about in the dining-room. There was a bowl of red and gold nasturtiums and a starched white cloth on the table and everything set out pleasantly with a kind of dew freshness for the midday meal. Aletta made things feel that way.

'Here you are at last,' she called. 'What a long time you have been, Franz.'

'I shall eat later. Crows are worrying the lambs and I am going after them.'

He went through the lounge and was taking down his rifle from the gun-rack in the passage when she came from the dining-room. Rooi was at her heels.

He slipped a clip of soft-nosed bullets in his pocket. 'Damn those crows. They would trouble me just now!' he muttered, glancing down his cheek at her.

'Franz, what are you doing?'

'I told you I was going after the crows!' He was already half-way out to the stoep and shouted back at her. And he hurried on and whistled to the dog. Rooi looked up once at Aletta and then raced out. But on the path he stopped and raised one front paw in hesitation.

'Come, Rooi! Sa, sa, sa! Hasies!' Franz called.

Aletta took the things off the table and put the meat-dish with a lid over it in the warming oven to keep for Franz. She had a queer feeling all the while going about the house and arranging things. The maid watched her aslant.

'Ai, my nonna, what is the basie doing?' the girl suddenly asked.

Aletta was bending over a camphor chest sorting and putting away the newly-ironed linen. And she remained quite still. So the Kafir maid knew there was something wrong. Her heart was gripped, seared with a jet of anger. What right had this girl to ask, what right to interpose one spoken word between her and Franz? She was black, a thing of instincts, and she had guessed somewhere in her dark soul that the white people were walking in fear. A crack had opened under their feet.

'Go out, Beta.' She had a husk in her throat trying to control her voice and did not turn. 'Go out and clean the chicken-hokkie.'

The girl went and Aletta was alone in the house. She walked to the window and looked out. Beyond the near-

145

black column of the cypress was the slope of the bush-dotted valley, close and hot, dropping away in haze. And then far off were the hills, crest behind crest of deepening blues to the peaks on the skyline, without snow but looking unattainable and cold under the pulsing ash-blue sky. It was unsettling to see so far – she knew that now. The distance stole like a restless wind into one's heart and gave one no peace. She had made a mistake hacking through the old shaggy trees of the Boer homestead, bursting out a window on the outside. Better for one's peace to build the walls up higher, let the woods grow denser, thicker, closing round the loneliness of a single spirit, shutting out the unbearable winds of the great world. She and Franz had failed to find any firm centre; the farm provided them, but could not contain nor hold them in its essential rhythm of work; and now that they were tested there seemed nothing left, no escape. They could get away if they were together, like truants, for a time. But they had to come back, to reality. Better if Franz had been strong, stronger than she like his father Christiaan, though his gentleness and good nature, his lack of ambition or greed had been so attractive. He was so generous, trusting.

She went back to the kitchen and walked about the house seeing nothing, but automatically shifting a vase of flowers and pushing back a curtain. Then she deliberately changed into rubber-soled walking-shoes and put on a neat little hat and dark glasses. She was going to find Franz.

Aletta heard a noise on the stoep, shuffling, a chair being moved. She thought with a new flicker of anger it was the maid come back to pry into her secrets. She walked out firmly, through the lounge and out at the glass doors. It was not the maid on the stoep, it was Rooi. He was lying on the green paving, one foreleg had been shattered above the elbow joint by a bullet and he was slowly licking the wound while the blood welled gradually out in a puddle near him. Franz had shot him – she saw at a glance – and failed to kill him.

She stood in the doorway, her heart bursting, and her tears came in a rush.

'Rooi, Rooi, oh, Rooi!' she sobbed, going forward to him. 'What am I going to do?'

The dog growled.

She was shaken with crying now, bitter within her, and knelt by him trembling. He let her stroke his head, but when she tried to touch the shattered leg, to stanch the blood with her handkerchief, he showed his teeth red with his own blood in a snarl. 'What am I to do?' she cried, and she was thinking of Franz.

She had no medical knowledge and could think of nothing but to stroke the dog's head while it went on stoically licking that awful wound.

She heard Franz coming, his footsteps rapid on the path, and her heart died in her. He was up the steps in a bound; she remained kneeling over the dog and felt him behind her, his presence like a weight on her.

'Aletta, it was an accident,' were his first words. He had to lie to her, now, of all times; he was so craven and weak. 'I shot at a crow on the koppie and the ricochet hit him. Ag, it was terrible, he went straight for home on three legs. . . . Speak to me, Aletta, for God's sake. You don't believe me!'

She shook her head.

He slammed down the rifle and dropped on one knee at her side. 'Why don't you talk to me, Aletta? God, God, say something. You must believe me.'

The dog had stopped licking its wound, raised its head balefully and growled as it had done when she first approached it. To Franz the growl came as a fearful shock. He stared open-mouthed and deadly white into the pain-deadened eyes of the animal. It was accusing him, as she was. She had turned against him as if she herself had been struck and the bullet was flying on . . . on . . . mowing down every dream and hope of his life. He found he was staring at the shattered leg, the wound and the blood pool on the tiles. Sickened, he stood up, and without thinking stretched out and took the gun. Aletta saw him, and in a moment was on her feet.

'Franz, are you mad? Put that gun down!'

He faced her woodenly, and it seemed his brain had grown benumbed and refused to grasp the position he was in.

'Why do you speak to me like that?' he demanded stubbornly.

'Give me the gun, Franz – you have done enough harm already.'

'No, I won't then,' he answered.

She reached forward slowly for the rifle, expecting that after a moment of hesitation he would surrender it to her. But he made no move, and she in her pain and grief and pity failed to see how shattered he was inside. She grasped the gun and he let it go. But her action had sparked off a sudden rage in him and he snatched the muzzle with one hand. She struggled to keep hold, her fingers slipping cruelly over the sharp metalwork as he jerked. Then there was a momentary pause as they faced one another in flaring anger, oblivious of all else. And she shifted her hold and the gun went off in her hands. Franz's fingers relaxed quite slowly and he went over to the wall and slid down it in a heap.

In the night she went back to where he was lying and put out the lamp and sat beside him. The neighbours had come and some were moving about the house and others talked low in her lounge. One of the farmers had put Rooi out of his suffering and they buried him under the flagstone at the foot of the cypress. The older women had laid Franz out and dressed him in his best suit and crossed his hands over his breast. She was weeping subduedly as she sat near him seeing his face in the dimness of their room. But there was a strange quiet acceptance far down in her soul. There had been no escape for them, no escape, no escape. And she had lost him at the moment they had found it out.

'My darling, my darling,' she whispered. 'Why did it have to be you?' And she remembered how dead he had looked last night as if in a grim, unread wish, while now he seemed merely in a deep and unutterably peaceful sleep.

It was before sunrise. Hendrik Gonzalez was scrubbing down the little white deck of the boat, and she watched him at work. He kept his face averted, shy and young. In his movements was a curious absorption, a completeness as if each action had its precise rhythm, a harmonic of his fundamental living tone. She knew he was instinctively musical, and it seemed natural to see his unusual balance in those terms. He had on a blue, short-sleeved vest and tight faded denims rolled up to the knee. His thick black hair was too long, untidy, and he shook it from his face with a slight, easy movement. Gonzalez – of Portuguese origin, or the name could as well have come to him like other accidents in the mystery of his past. He would be inconspicuous in any of the hot fishing harbours of the Mediterranean, brown, small-boned, but with an ancient physical delicacy, a power beyond himself. And yet he was far removed from the Old World, a coloured boy who had drifted from the country of the Western Cape to become a fisherman at Saldanha Bay.

They heard two rapid shots, a left-right of a sporting-gun, and he half turned, looking not at her, but to one side over the stern of the boat.

'He has hit this time maybe, Mevrou.' He did not smile, though his eyes were mocking. Then he raised his dark glance to follow the birds wheeling and crying above the enormous quiet surface of the bay and the grey sand-dunes dotted with tough little desert bushes. She said nothing but followed his look. As the gulls flew up from the grey water higher and higher into the sky they threw back suddenly an astonishing metallic gleam, a flash, turning on black-tipped wings into the level rays of the coming sun.

'How wonderful,' she said.

'They are first in the sun,' he said, and looked to the east above the low black hills beyond the sand-dunes. The sky shaded from orange and pink to a lustrous dome of blue, cloudless. All round the horizon were the softening colour layers, salmon and pale heliotrope merged into fire blue. In a few minutes all would disappear under the white, throbbing, brilliant African day. He stood leaning on the broom a moment and then went on scrubbing, his head to one side. She stepped across to the planks of the jetty to collect the things sent down from the house for the day's boat-trip. When she stood up she saw the man with the gun coming at a distance along the edge of the bay. The gun was across his shoulder and a brown and white spaniel followed him. Sunlight was touching the factory roofs, it crept down the boat masts and soon she felt the flush of pleasant warmth on her neck. She turned full face into the sun, smiling, creasing her wide, light-blue eyes.

She had turned away from the man with his dog and sporting-gun to face into the sunlight, and with her smile of pleasure the lines smoothed gradually out of her forehead. Unthinkingly she loosened the clip and shook out her soft, brown hair. There was one perfect time of the day here, the half-hour before and after sunrise. She could imagine how, gazing over a like sunrise on the Mesopotamian desert, men had seen their pattern of the Creation. They had witnessed the unfolding of a lordly earth out of chaos. She, a northerner, blonde, from the little nation of

Holland, clinging with bare nails to the watery edge of a cold continent, she had felt her heart expand to Africa, the sun, the desert, until she had slowly grown aware within herself of an unknown and disturbing person. For this one hour she wanted to be left in peace, with the strong melon-scented sea water, the birds, the surrounding desert; and with Hendrik Gonzalez, too, since he was a part of it; he might well have been part of the Creation itself, simple and alive, still ignorant, wondering but smiling at the earth. The way he had said: 'They are first in the sun,' as if he loved the birds for their marvellous daring, and did not envy them.

'Hello, Mariana,' the man called.

'Oh, hello, Philip.'

'You're up early.'

He came nearer, his grey eyes flickering in a familiar smile. He had a war scar that drew up his right eyelid at the corner and made him look more provocative, restless. His lips were red and moist and he had a short reddish moustache, his skin very sunburnt and peeling. He looked English, prodigiously, amusingly English; almost unbeliev-able there on the barren coast, tall with a high-bridged nose and hard chin and his clothes in careless good taste except for the loose rawhide velskoens. He was a generation removed from England. South Africa had reared and developed him, white South Africa, leaving him oddly incomplete with a kind of blank at the back of his mentality.

'I missed,' he said. 'A sand-piper flying a real crazy zigzag. Wonderful practise really, those birds.'

'Are you going up to the hotel?'

He came close to her, smiling warily, and put the shot-gun butt down between his feet. 'You're not going out in the boat, are you?'

'I am, of course, and I shall wait for you. But please don't keep me long.'

'Not today, Mariana. My directors are coming down from Cape Town.'

'Oh, then I shall go alone.'

'Your husband's coming down too.'

'I know.'

'And you're not waiting to see him?'

'No,' she answered, without raising her eyes. 'He hates sailing. I'll go now if you can't come.'

'Don't be silly – not alone.'

'With Hendrik, of course.'

'But, Mariana, he's clueless. What if the wind gets up stronger than usual?'

'We can put up a sail and come romping home.'

'Which sail?'

She glanced impatiently at him and gathered up the basket and parcels and the two short fishing-rods with large-size American reels.

'Mariana,' he said, suddenly tense and dropping the stubborn, enduring outer shell he wore habitually. 'I mean this – can't we hoist sail and head slap out into the ocean, to Tristan da Cunha, or Rio, or the Gulf of Mexico. It's being done every day, why not by us? The boat's as sturdy as a tree. All we need is water and three months' supplies.'

'Wonderful,' she said. He had followed her aboard and she leaned against the low deck-house facing him. 'Get finished with your directors and with Frikkie and we can take a sail round to Cape Columbine tomorrow.'

'Cape Columbine be blowed. Mariana, I'm serious. What's to stop us sailing out west away from all this; just you and I.'

'And what about our deck-hand, Hendrik?'

'He would never venture out of sight of land.'

'Nor would I, Philip. It's a healthy instinct. Well, the sun will soon be getting hot. Help me cast off, Philip.'

He made no move. The smile came back on his lips and danced in that provocative eye, a steel-hard shielding smile.

'Mariana, can you guess why my directors and Frikkie and his lot are all bundling down here today?'

'If it's business, I can't guess; I don't want to know, really. And they are not coming for a picnic, are they?'

'No.' He was gazing at her with a twitch of his lips. She spoke perfect English, but with a wholly lovable accent which gave her speech precision yet sounded as if her mouth had in it some small, soft membrane muting the sharpness of a foreign tongue.

'I don't care either,' he said. 'I could do anything. I could send them all to hell, if only I was sure of you, Mariana.'

'Why, don't you feel sure?'

'You never let me.'

'Philip, I love you more than I love anyone else. You know I don't care about Frikkie.'

'And he, does he know?'

She had ducked into the little cabin to tidy away things and came up, leaning her elbows on the companion-rails.

'Something is wrong with you, something awful. We have never asked questions, we have never made confessions. No. Between us we have been free. But now, Philip, you sound like a small boy, afraid. You are in a panic.'

He laughed, lifting the gun across his shoulders. The spaniel stayed on the jetty, shuddering from nose to tail with anxiety and watching his slightest move. Gonzalez was up in the bows on his haunches deftly polishing the brass.

'Well, good-bye,' Philip said, and held out a hand. She put her hand in his.

'But what is this – why good-bye?'

'Wish me luck, anyway.'

'Of course I do, Philip.'

'Against your husband?'

'Now you are being a small boy again. Philip, if you mix with man-eaters you know what to expect. No, I won't wish you luck against him. But if you are still alive and not eaten up tomorrow, come sailing to Cape Columbine.'

'Tomorrow. And tonight you will have the company of the excellent and successful Frikkie. I may be his employee by then, obliged to ask his permission for a day off with his wife. Or I may be out on my ear.'

She had lowered herself into the cabin and was so long there he thought she had not heard. He stepped back to the jetty planks and the dog jumped up eagerly, fawning on him. She bobbed out to wave, her face a creamy brown tan with a natural freshness in her cheeks, a Northern freshness, and round white teeth.

'Good luck, Philip!'

'I need it,' he called back, and the muscles of his face answered, imperfectly, with a ghastly smile. She watched him go, one hand in his pocket, the other hung across the gun-stock and the barrels aslant his shoulder gleaming blue in the sun. His back was slender and straight like a boy's, but he swung along ungainly, and slapped down the raw-hide velskoens in an aimless manner among the small pebbles and shells and the scrunching sand. She felt against him a hot centre of fury. He needed protection, and she could not feel protective; he seemed to have come to her like a child, only to leave her dismayed at the bewildering lack within her, the lack of feminine tenderness. She dreaded she, too, was petrifying, and when she felt down in her heart for a flower she would find a Kalahari rose, the perfect form of a rose left by the fine chiselling of the desert sand, but not a rose at all, scentless, lifeless, a thing of soft crumbling stone. Was she going that way too?

He had forgotten to help her cast off and Hendrik started the auxiliary motor and slipped the moorings himself. The bows swung slowly out until he let in the gear. The craft gave a little thrill of life and she felt the wheel answer. A small gull dipped close over her head in a salute of unexpressed joy and she could see for a moment its beautiful ruby-red bill glowing in the sunlight as if suffused with translucent blood. Ripples lapped under the bows. Hendrik was busy with the mainsail which they would hoist when they met the first wind. He leaned on the bulging canvas along the boom unhurriedly loosening the ties.

The boat skimmed on with the little engine muttering evenly and a slight sway of the mast. The water surface was filmy with the sub-visual life of uncountable sea organisms, and at intervals a big sheen-pink jellyfish undulated on its blind course. Foam patches sailed by. The sun was now throwing down big irregular stampings of pure gold on the sea and Mariana narrowed her eyes like a fishing skipper and scanned calmly the whole lazy expanse receding into colourless, opaque density at its farthest. There was twenty miles of uninterrupted sailing inside the land-locked bay, and off to the west was the wide opening to the Atlantic, low rocky islands, and the ocean murmuring, cold, restless, grey-blue.

'No fish,' she said to Gonzalez.

He looked up and pointed off the bow. 'A shoal there, Mevrou, maasbankers or haarders.'

She saw now the sea-birds converging on an air circus a mile off; a flight of black cormorants skimmed like a great arrow-head low over the boat, their hooked wings hissing with speed. Small shoal-fish were merely a good sign, no more. The bigger game would be somewhere about, off the islands or way out in the open.

Hendrik slowed down the motor until it was barely turning over, coughing water from the cooling pipe and sending smoke in wisps over the surface. She could see what he was preparing for. The morning breeze was coming across from the desert hills and sand-dunes. Like frost, like a shiver under an unexpected cold hand, the sea face wrinkled and drew into itself and shook with a dark sigh. She secured the wheel and climbed out quickly, and together they hauled up the big red-and-white striped mainsail. The canvas filled softly as if with light, not air, and a rich glow streamed down over them and on the deck and sea. The head turned a few points out towards the ocean and then the first full puff caught the sail and the little boat dipped, almost leaping for the endless freedom of the open West.

Hendrik Gonzalez was clueless with a boat, Philip said. He got flustered when given orders in yachting terms. But left to himself, he knew what to do and she gave no orders; she did what happened next, she fished or sunbathed or sailed or simply drifted in a lolling oily trough, and she knew he was watching with piercing eyes like a sea eagle all three elements, the grey-toothed treacherous desert coast that he never let out of his sight, the water and the clouds. He was always one move ahead of the elements.

The wind they had caught was a land-breeze born of the desert, and it had in it the smell of sleeping sand, the morning dew quickly sucked up and the bitter edge of arid herbs. It blew over tiny hamlets with a well and clay huts, but no trees, and over parched little fishing villages. It smelt of them, their desolation. It blew over the cramped grave-yards where the dead slept dry under a ring of crumbled whitening pearl-shells and rock crystals – waterless flowers in the white sand. She tried to think of life in a village like that, of growing up, manhood and womanhood.

'What part of the country do you come from?' she asked her deck-hand, who was laying out fishing tackle on the fore-deck. He turned his head like a wild animal stopped in its tracks by a suspicious sound. His glance slid across her face and beyond to the land. There was deference in those eyes, but also, she thought, a streak of insolence. He was proud in his own way, proud of his acquired skill on the water, of his success with the factory girls. Insolence was a substitute for dignity in the face of the white race, yet the subconscious dignity was there all the time, in his strength and manhood and youth and in the balance and harmony of him pitted against the elements. He lifted a hand in a short gesture, speaking quietly.

'My home is there, Mevrou. But a long way, over the Cold Bokkeveld Mountains. Mevrou would not know the place.'

He was not inviting more questions about himself.

'You have learnt to be a fisherman then, instead of a farm-hand. Have you been far out to sea?'

'Far enough, Mevrou. Beyond that is the grave of the white sailors.'

'Why do you say that?'

'Many ships, many lives have been lost there, they say.

The women who go to collect feather-down of the malmocks blown up from the sea on to the beaches sometimes find the bone of a drowned man there.'

'The sea is full of death, but you are not afraid when you are on it.'

'No.'

'If you know the presence of death and you see the workings of death and you live in the mercy of being spared, then it loses its terror. But when you live with a hole in your heart and something unknown up against the hills, something that is always behind you, then you turn into something fear-ridden like a man with a secret cancer. You become a partner of death, destructive.'

'Mevrou?' he said, frowning, puzzled. Then he turned away and went on with his work, colouring darkly as if a door had been slammed in his face. She was no longer talking to him.

She felt exultant holding the boat into the wind, its whole frame vibrating gently, eager and joyful, the gold on the ripples and, funnelled down the big sheet of the sail, a ruddy fall of light. It was her husband's boat; she had got him to buy it, and he had sailed in it once only. He was sea-sick and hated it. They had bought it six weeks ago, and of that time she had spent every week except one at Saldanha, loving the boat, the sea and the intoxicating freedom they shared. Her seaside house was built of white crumbly sandstone, two former fishermen's cottages joined together, enlarged and modernised, but retaining something primitive – the ceilings of smoke-darkened polished bamboos, an old-fashioned bake-oven and pot-hooks and roasting-spit in the kitchen. She had the floors done with Dutch tiles and put blue Dutch china on the dresser shelves. Her husband was not a sensitive man, but he had the delicacy to leave her to herself. She knew it would not last, and she felt as she had in Holland when a child of eleven on the eve of war, tantalised, excited but resigned to the unknown.

She met Frikkie after Holland was liberated; he was then an Air Force lieutenant, handsome with his dark, burnt skin and violet-blue eyes, a rather long face, droll and irresponsible as if he were always ready with a joke against each new absurdity. He did think things were absurd, especially the stuffiness of old Europe that everybody was busy crawling back into after the upheaval. Holland was amusing, and to him was no more his mother country than was Japan, although he spoke Afrikaans, a close relative of Hollands. She was sixteen, slender, bright-eyed and hurt deeply in her consciousness by the occupation, the treachery and suspicion and the awful denial of freedom. She had seen Frikkie as a gay knight-errant, an emanation from the far world of sun and freedom, broadness, broad horizons, distance, toleration after the little cold concentration camp of her native Holland.

She lavished on him an unconditional worship, measureless and generous as only a child's love could be. They were married in South Africa two years later, and she began to see him at work as a civilian. He had a science degree, but he was muscling into business. Two passions absorbed him, an old childhood love of things mechanical and, transforming and reacting on it, an almost insane material ambition. He read and seemed to enjoy books of popular mathematics. For hours he would sit toying with an outsize slide-rule, calculating, calculating, calculating, and always there would be a half-smile on his handsome but droll face as if he found an intense fascination and enchantment in the precision of symbols. She lost track of his interests and pursuits and his involvement in the financial side of affairs. This was a time when she was discovering herself and simultaneously Frikkie and his associates. She had soon felt the incongruity of thinking of Africa, or South Africa, as a land of free horizon, a 'young' country. It was neither; it was incredibly, primordially ancient and exclusive. Only what was ancient or instinctual belonged, merged integrally with the great sombrely glittering reality. Everything else was alien. The dark races belonged by a rhythm and sympathy that had nothing to do with what the world called civilisation. When they were at the pinnacles of civilisation they would still merge. It took an antelope perhaps millions of years to adapt its poise and colouring into the cycle, the throb of the bush-veld. And that ancestry was his claim, a title that could not be understood save by the most acute fineness of sense. A white woman might find the true harmonic, the vibration of Africa, because she was more instinctual, ancient and tender in her feelings, provided she was un-trammelled, not dominated by her males. But the white male was an alien. She could not explain it, but since the understanding had gestated within her she had watched and felt and had found no exception. The white males were alien. Most of the females were too, but the men remained insidiously apart, angled, unhappy.

She remembered seeing as a child in Holland an art book with a strange and shocking reproduction of a canvas by some South American painter whose name she had for-gotten. It was the head of a young man in profile with large feeling eyes, soft mouth and a brow lined subtly with in-comprehension, as if he failed quite to grasp some thought. And everything about the head was full, alive and perceptive

F

THE TAME OX

except that the artist had painted the back of the skull open and empty. The bone cut away and the brain matter visible but scooped out. And the face giving no indication that he knew what was missing.

To her, Frikkie was like that. Some part of his brain which he had been gifted with at birth had gone dead, smashed up or severed or withered from disuse. The rest of the brain was terribly alive, virulent, avid. But he was not a whole person, and once you knew you always waited for his thought to run into that dead hollow like a train skipping the rails. Others were like that; she began to judge men by how much she thought was lost, Frikkie's business friends, the set they mixed with at parties and dances and official functions. All of them had a point like a notch on a steam-gauge when their eyes suddenly went blank. They were no more capable of thought because there was nothing left to think with, just the hole, the pulp. Sometimes she would see it or imagine it when she read about things that happened; big, gentle and unroused men brought to a dead stop, and then the rise of fear like impure blood in the neck arteries, the quick turn of the head like a snake's to deceit, violence, panic.

She had also seen streams of her own people passing through Cape Town after the Dutch pulled out of the East Indies. They were white men, Dutchmen, but you could not call them Europeans, they were so incomplete, so damaged. In a way, they were like the white males of South Africa. She wondered if this was the fate of the white man and his civilising misson, that in the end he lost his grip on his own values. Or was it merely the colonist, the master race, the *colon* regardless of race who consumed himself? Maybe the Romans had streamed back while their empire collapsed with just the same fury and incomprehension in their impaired brains as the Dutch out of Java, the English from India or the remnants of the *conquistadores* from the Americas.

Mariana had thought she had found the exception when she met Philip. He was a business man but a rebel, unorthodox in his methods, keen and impressionable about everything. He joked that his grandfather had owned a £25,000 pottery in Burslem. His father had made – and lost – £50,000 as a sugar planter in South Africa and there was nothing left for him to do but double up again. He started with a rock-lobster boat in the Cape waters, went on to own two little deck vessels and trawl nets and then switched into processing – canned and frozen sea foods, fish-meal, oils, fertilizer. His original and branch companies were nearing a capitalisation of £100,000.

'What will you do then?' somebody had asked him.

'Chuck the whole thing up and breed horses,' he said. He was a bachelor and lived on a small farm in an old gabled Dutch house he had repaired in faithful detail. She was enchanted with Philip and with his home, his collection of prints and paintings and old weapons. His only pose was that of an English gentleman. But he was too thin-skinned; he laughed at his own ideal for fear others would laugh first. On his boats, he worked like a deck-hand or mechanic. He stood over the factory machines or would slosh about among the fish-tanks in thigh-boots. His working clothes stank of fish. He lent his factory hands the company lorries for Sunday picnics and outings and went along with them to drink sherry and enjoy the fun. And yet, behind it all, was a gaping inadequacy. He could never 'chuck up' his business because he was too involved and his methods made him in-

efficient and vulnerable. He made no real or intimate con-
tact with his employees and felt always the ugly blank between himself and them. And with Mariana he was lost. He
lay with her, feeling the agony steal down into his soul that
she was coming to despise him, this lithe, smooth-skinned
intangible girl who looked at him solemnly but with a rising
impulse of laughter in the glistening light-blue of her eyes.
They did not discuss it, that was part of their convention.
But he felt with her like a glazed, desert insect whose wings
she could pluck off one by one from curiosity when she felt
inclined.

Frikkie, her husband, had been fascinated by Philip's
enterprise. He knew nothing about boats, fish or food-pack-
ing, but he got busy, probing, calculating. He saw Philip's
weak spots, his business inefficiency and his lack of capital,
and he was amused at his friendship with Mariana. He and
his associates went in with a rival company. They had back-
ing from a special finance corporation and they had plenty
of pull – permits, quotas, labour direction smoothed in
months the way Philip had trodden in years. They were
waiting to absorb the unorthodox amateur, and they knew
his limit was near. The final straw had been an official contract for fish-meal giving them effective control and laying
Philip's concern open to their pressure.

Mariana knew the broad drift of the matter and refused
to be concerned with details. She had no wish to be drawn
in, to save Philip or to intercede with her husband. Frikkie
was not acting from jealousy. He was a natural man-eater.
When he had swallowed Philip and his outfit he would turn
to something else and devour that. Most likely, she thought,
he would pull out of the fish business at a sizeable profit, sell
everything, the cottage and boat as well as the factories and

jettys and trawlers. Then she would be stranded again. She felt a pang about that, but about Philip she had a different feeling, a stab of guilt, of regret that she found no desire, no tenderness to shelter him in. When she said she loved him he knew all the while it was to soothe, a touch of salve, leaving the torment to rage deep in his breast.

The wind was blowing up more briskly and Gonzalez moved back to help her take in the sail. They were passing the low rocky headland about a mile to windward and the boat was leaping the easy swell like a beautiful bird.

'Is Mevrou going to fish?' Gonzalez asked.

'No, I am going to sail. Will the wind last, Hendrik?'

'The wind will last and it is coming up stronger.'

'I am going down the wind and then beat back level with Vondeling Island and run in on the afternoon blow. I shall stay and fish at the turn if there's time.'

She wanted to sail out of sight of land and steer back by the compass, and she wondered from the cautious way he looked round if he had guessed her thoughts. He hauled up the jib, the canvas filled and they turned, racing down the sparkling path of the south-easter. She laughed aloud at the exhilaration of surging movement.

'Could you throw out a spoon in case of tunny,' she called. She watched Hendrik pay out a few fathoms of line and secure the reel. Turning, she could see through the green water of the boat's wake a glint of the sun on the silver spinning lure.

'Do you go out again tonight?'

'Yes, Mevrou, trekking,' he answered, standing against the mast and without looking at her. Trekking was net fishing inshore.

'Could I come trekking?'

'You could, Mevrou. But it may be unwise, dangerous.'

'What can be dangerous about it? You don't go out far.'

He did not answer, but watched the flicker of the rod.

'You mean women don't go trekking?'

'*Dis gevaarlik*,' he repeated his warning of danger.

'Well, I am not afraid. I'm sailing out of sight of land today, over the grave of the white sailors. Do you mind?'

He shook his head.

'Can you swim?'

'I cannot swim, Mevrou.'

'Why don't you learn – you are a fisherman.' But he merely shrugged in perfect indifference. He sat down with his back to the mast and his small dark feet drawn up together. The wind ruffled his black hair and blew lank strands across his eyes.

They sailed on and the land went down into a reddish gauzy band between the sea and the sky. She asked him to take the wheel, and went up and stretched out on the forward deck. She had on a brief sun-suit and her back and legs were exposed to the sun. Pressing down her breasts she felt the warmth of the scrubbed planks strike through the thin print, like the warmth of a man's body. But the ship was female – people called it that, 'she'. Mariana loved the little craft, could it be an unnatural love? She smiled. No, a ship was of all things conceived by man the most masculine, wholly virile, a supple vaulting splendour infused with pure spirit. Maybe the placid rush boats of Egyptian papyri were female, but the tall-masted craft of the North was all male. She was in love with the sea itself and its dwellers. The sea could never be conquered, it was too wily and ancient, too patient, cruel. Africa was like that, all the while striking back secretly at its would-be dominators, finally unconquerable. First into the dawn through the deep-back millenia of the Pharoahs, it would also be last in the evening of man and woman, their life cradle and their bier. That was the germ of what she had begun to discover. She wanted her dreams and her daring, she wanted to be free and to be left in peace in that hour of creation announced by the rising sun. Turning, she could see in the angle of her eye the swift curves of the big sail, red and white against the distilled blue fire of the sky. She rolled back her head on her arms and fell asleep.

Mariana did not know if they had sailed over the grave of the white sailors, out of sight of land. She woke to find Hendrik Gonzalez had brought the boat to in sight of a rocky island with a squat red-and-black lighthouse.

'But that's Dassen Island!' she said, amazed.

'You slept a long time, Mevrou.'

'We are miles and miles south, how ever did we get here?'

'The boat sailed, Mevrou.'

'My God, and I missed it. Was it wonderful?'

'The wind got up strong and I came round.' He swept his arm in a curve. 'Now it has turned south and we can get home without the engine.'

'That's good. Have you caught any fish?'

'No fish. If Mevrou wants to fish now I will bait a line, there are perhaps snoek running.'

'I'll sail, and I want to get something to eat. You get on with the fishing.'

She turned the boat before the light southerly breeze and they both settled to the routine of the voyage home. She felt drowsy, full of content. Her skin tingled, and with her even heart-beats she felt inwardly the blood ripple in her neck and down her stomach and thighs. Tiny needle-points of light sparked in her eyes. After half an hour Hendrik cried out: 'Hey skelm!'

He reeled in one of the lines and a long slender fish, silver and gleaming with black and purple, was swung on to the deck, snapping vicious jaws. He clubbed the snoek deftly and threw it in a fish-basket. He did not glance at her and she turned to check the course. The sun was a quarter angle over the sea. They should, if all went well, make the jetty and home before it set.

Later, the wind failed, and it was after dark when they came in. Fishermen helped them tie up and took off Hendrik's catch of snoek. At the cottage she found a note from Frikkie; they were keeping dinner for her at the hotel. She had dressed when she heard his car sweep round the gravel outside. He came in flushed and excited, his long droll face printed with an ineradicable smile. There was a brightness in his deep-blue eyes, attractive perhaps, except that he had been drinking and the lines of his skin were strained, dissolute. They talked, on the way to the hotel, about the boat and the day's trip.

The dinner-party took up all of the small main dining-room. The directors were there from both sides, Frikkie's people and Philip's. Some had brought their wives for the day's outing. The factory managers and a few others Mariana did not know lined up to wait for their places. Philip looked like a high school Rugby captain who has lost his match and broken a knee, but is smiling bloodlessly through the wreck of his dreams. She was suddenly nauseated and bitterly angry. The way his eyes sought hers across the room like a beaten dog, the drawn smile. Her forehead seemed to go icy cold. Why did he take his thrashing like this, why not send them to hell, as he had said? There they all were, lumpy, preposterous half-men, and he in his terrible thin skin quivering with pain. They were waiting for Frikkie to get at the table. He was the hero of the evening, he had the right pull, he had their money safe enough in his control. They bunched about, humoured him and roared at his drolleries. She went round to Philip, calmer now, and looked directly but softly into his eyes.

'I'm sorry, Philip.'

'It's all right.'

'Is that all you want to say? I know you are hurt, Philip, but you're not blaming me, are you?'

'Why should I?'

'You said if you were sure about me . . .'

'I'm sure.'

She was frightened for a moment, wondering what he meant. His voice sounded so battered and hollow.

'Philip, why do you stay here and let them tear the flesh off your bones? Look at them, they are lizards, alligators. And Frikkie, tonight he's all evil to his marrow. You can't stay, Philip.'

'I will. I'll show them.'

'My God,' she said, feeling sick.

Hendrik Gonzalez sat on the step outside the kitchen door of the hotel. It was late, almost midnight by the wheel of the stars. He was waiting for two serving men and the wine steward to make up his boat-crew for the trekking. Plenty of time, all the ages before dawn. But they would be a little tired rushing to and fro, waiting on the white people. He had seen his mevrou leave earlier in the evening. She took her husband's car and drove herself down to the cottage, although it was only five minutes' walk. White women were like she-leopards, full of terror and savagery, they valued themselves highly even if they were ugly old bones in a sack of skin. But she was not like that, she was not simply another in the run of white women. She was a foreigner, proud and high in her own right, an *ulanner*, aristocrat. Yet how could you explain her wanting to come and trek fish with a boat-load of rough men? Or what was more, her choice of a husband. Women were beyond understanding.

He had his mandolin across his knees and plucked muted notes from it with the soft of his thumb. He sang quietly a song about a Cape girl with her hair in plaits and bells at her ankles.

The Englishman came out of the hotel alone and walked off; tall and straight he looked against the skyline in the light of the stars with his gun across one shoulder. What was he going to shoot at night – a dikkop perhaps? But how could one tell where the dikkops flew except by their sad baby-like cry which seemed to drop out of the stars themselves? The Englishman was crazy.

A little later the three men of his boat crew came out at the kitchen door and Hendrik Gonzalez stood up, stretching. One of them handed him a half-bottle of sherry which he slid into the inner pocket of his jacket.

'Come,' he said, hitching the cord of the mandolin on his shoulder. They took the path to the bay in single file, Gonzalez picking a tune on sharp strings and the others humming. From the hotel behind them they heard a burst of laughter.

'Ag, they spend money like water, but with their tips they are mean,' the wine steward said. Their feet raked into the shelly gravel, going down. As they passed some distance below Frikkie's cottage the curtains of a window were thrown open and they could see the outline of the white woman against the shine of an oil-lamp. Then the lamp was blown out and Gonzalez was almost sure he saw the pale shape of the girl again in the black window-frame. But it could be a trick of his eyes. The stars seemed to sway like leaves on fire in the enormous black trees of a forest.

They took the pole across their shoulders and slid the boat down the sand and shingle until it was borne up by the cold water. One by one they jumped in and began putting out the oars. The net was piled in a great black heap in the stern with the cork floats faintly visible like a row of toy train wheels.

'Ready,' Hendrik called.

Across the desert sands beside the bay came a single shot.

'Ai!' he said, resting forward on the oar. 'That is the mad Englishman.'

'What's he shooting?'

'No, it is not like him at all. He always fires bam-bam – left and right. I thought he might be after dikkop.'

'But who could see a dikkop in the dark?'

'Ag, then he must have shot himself.'

'*Toe maar!*' another of the three reproved him mildly.

Gonzalez dipped his oar and pulled a long, gentle sweep, and when he raised it from the black surface, it sheered into the air with a broad flash of phosphorescence, scattering drops like fiery quicksilver.

'Ah, that's lucky,' one of the serving men sang out, a touch of rapture in his voice, running out his oar with a rumble through the iron ring. 'That's a lucky sign for us, I say – lucky.'

STONEWALL'S GHOST

Kleinhans stepped along in the rough white sand and white pebbles and whitened limey shells. The glare hurt his eyes. He was pale and there was a transparent blueness around his eye-sockets, but his lips were red, burning and dry. His faded blue shirt had a big rip in the back and he wore khaki pants frayed at the bottom – then a stretch of wiry sun-peeling ankles down to the small feet slipping about in over-size rawhide velskoens. The cold wind that always got up off the sea in the afternoons flapped his clothes. He pulled down the peak cap hard and hugged his arms over his chest.

He was coming along the shore path under the low head-land and making for the village. Ahead of him the rocks ran down a jag towards the beach, and once beyond the point he would come in sight of the fishing harbour at the head of the bay and above it the village. The sea was slatey and opaque under wind gusts, sunlight flashed big glints off the turning rollers and struck colours in the blown spray. He felt the spray cold on his skin and the wind was cold, but the sun behind him pushed a warm finger through the hole in his shirt and touched his neck. He halted, seeing someone on the path down at the point. He knew who it was of course, and it was too late to go back, so he screwed up his shoulders a little and went on.

When he came up she just said gently: 'Kleinhans.' He glanced at her aslant. 'Middag, Alida,' he answered, stepping aside from the path but going on. She had been gathering coral sea-weed, a few big fan-shaped pieces of the marvellous sea pattern, red and mauve-pink, that tourists liked.

'Where are you off to, Kleinhans?'

'The village.' He jerked his head in that direction.

'Not to the harbour?'

He stopped and half turned. Still hugging his chest, he could feel how his heart slugged, and now he coloured up hot. 'You know damn well where I'm going – All right, I'll say it. I'm going to the canteen and I'm going to drink until my money's finished, or till they throw me out on the beach, whichever's first. And I hope that pleases you – the lot you care.'

'You have no right to say that, Kleinhans.'

'I have said it then, and can I go catch my words back out of the air?' He laughed and began coughing heavily.

'O Lord God, what a torment it is you bring down on yourself and everyone near. Kleinhans van As, you could be a boat-owner and the leading man here one day – but look at you. . . .'

'Ja, look at me.'

'You make enemies of everyone, you would drive the dear Jesus out of your own heart.'

'Forget about it,' he said, 'I have got my friends.'

He walked on and she looked after him. She was eighteen and she had left Kleinhans. She was going to marry Willie Momsen and she should not have said that about boat-owners. Willie had taken over the fishing-boat *Malmok* when Kleinhans could not keep up the payments. It had been a fair deal and the boatmen reckoned Kleinhans had been well treated, considering. The *Malmok* was the most beautiful craft in the southern sea, and it was like the bird it was named for. Norwegians had made it and there was not an unsound fibre in all its length and beam. Down to the last cleat and nail it was a thing of pride. They had sailed it half round the world – its engine never missed a beat and it laughed at storms. Kleinhans had bought the *Malmok* on good terms at Walvis. His loss of it had not been the first blow, but the last. He had made men turn their back on him, he had fought and brawled and jeered at the meaner types and at skippers and owners up and down the coast. He had wanted to take Alida to the west with him, but her father stopped it. And when he got back she would not see him. He knew why, of course. Willie Momsen was nothing to her. She was taken to an aunt on a farm near Treurfontein and Momsen went to see her there in his car. You could not sail the *Malmok* over the mountains to Treurfontein. A thousand times in his heart he had said: 'To hell with her.'

Instead of going up to the village he kept to the shore, following the white curve of the bay. She watched him until his figure got lost behind some of the older thatched cottages where there were long wooden frames of fish-drying stellasies with the bunches of silver doppies and flecked yellowtail and snoek out in the sun and salt. Beyond that were sheds and the cove where the boats had once been pulled up out of the open seas. Then the wall and pier of the new harbour and the big square patch of calm water full of every kind of small craft moored alongside or anchored at the buoys. In the middle of the harbour at its own buoy and a proud distance from any other was the white and pale grey hull of the *Malmok*, with touches of blue on its funnel and life-belts.

Kleinhans could see the *Malmok*, too, as he went along,

disappearing and bobbing up. It hurt him to look, but he needed that. It was a hook in his guts. He felt Alida's grey eyes under the sun-bonnet would be on him and deliberaately he went on without turning. He could still get her back – why had she come out on the path? She knew he was living at Groenewald's tumbledown place at Mosselklip. Willie Momsen was away in Cape Town on some business trip and would not be back until late. Willie skippered his own boats and would skin-dive with the men for abalone (called perlemoen along the coast), but he was the kind who never took a chance. He never went down without full kit, an air-pipe and compressor and a second diver alongside in case of accident. Now Willie was using *Malmok* as his 'flag-ship'. He skippered her and had two other boats. Maybe the price of getting Alida back was to be respectable, a boat-owner, and for that matter he did not give a damn.

When he got to the skeleton of an old wrecked boat-hull half down in the sand, Kleinhans stopped. He wanted a drink and he would have it later – she was not stopping him. But meanwhile he did what he liked. He found a place where the boat timbers made a shelter against the wind and the sun beat down hot on the sand. First he sat there, back to the wreck; then rolled over on his stomach and lay full out with his face on his arms.

He pretended to be asleep hearing footsteps come quietly up to him in the sand. They stopped, and whoever it was remained near-by, silent. He guessed who had come; nobody else around the place would come singling him out except to risk a snarling quarrel or a fight. Presently he opened one eye and looked from below his cap brim. First one voice said: 'Bwana!' And then another, deeper voice followed.

Slowly he coiled himself up again and sat in the hot sand
hugging his knees. Without thinking at first he smiled into
the two bronze-black faces. 'Huh, Stonewall . . . huh, Jefferson,' he said. They brought a wild, unfathomable feeling
into him, more than mere joy to him, active and surging
through his body. To the devil with everyone! Why
shouldn't they be so, man to man? They were life to him,
especially Stonewall. Not merely that Stonewall had saved
him from drowning, that was incidental. They would all
three do the same for the others, and they were bound
together by a disregard for their own lives that amounted
to a kind of mania, and absolute summing up and finality
of courage since it was unthought of and taken without
question. The two black men were 'brothers', they said.
That meant they were cousins or clansmen or maybe no
closer than belonging to the same sub-tribe. Chavimzaba
was their clan, and they had taken on new names – Stonewall and Jefferson – that gave them some sort of standing
with the whites. Both were small, slim, well-knit and their
faces grave, at rest, like black Arabs. They were not
Southern Bantu, but Nyasas from somewhere far inland on
the Central African lakes. They came south against all
chance, against the regulations and police vigilance, and
once they saw the blue ocean something happened in their
hearts that was like a young bird taking the freedom of the
sky. They became black hawks of the sea, Vikings. If a
skipper got a Nyasa 'boy' he hung on to him, he would break
laws, he would lie and shift for his sake. There were still
quite a few Nyasas about the boats and in the location back
among the sand-dunes. Kleinhans had not gone out of his
way to collect his two. They had come on the *Malmok* once
when he was preparing to go to sea, and with one look at

Stonewall his heart had jumped. He had not said a word, just a nod at the fo'c'sle cabin and they were as good as signed on. That night as he stood at the wheel and the Southern Cross blazed over his shoulder and Orion plunged head first towards the Atlantic, he had heard the Nyasas singing, and the tears suddenly streamed down into his beard. He felt shame that like a woman he could be moved by other men's sadness. Yet he was glad too. It was no ordinary sorrow that wandered from them over the ocean, but a strong burning of men's hearts.

That was what he meant when he told Alida he had his friends. He would not say who they were. Maybe she would understand, maybe not. A woman, even a young girl like her, would see things that were closed off against other eyes, while sometimes being blind to the naked and obvious truth. But to anyone else – God! he knew what they would say. Stonewall and Jefferson themselves would be overcome with shame if he blundered out with any words of friendship or affection. Stonewall particularly. He was like a small, alert night creature, delicate to every sound and sense. He certainly knew how firm and clear was the bond between them and his high standard of pride made it a law that he acted well once his allegiance was given.

'I am not going out,' Kleinhans said at last. The two men squatting in the sand made a faint sighing sound of disappointment.

'Baas Swart's boat is ready. We put tar in the leak. We put kit with boat. Ready to fish.'

'Listen to me, Stonewall – for the last time——'

'Haa.' The soft sound and a wounded look in his black slope eyes.

'I am not sweating in a bloody hired boat with a motor

178

that's not worth a tin can. I can't pick my fishing-ground, I can't get far enough to beat the others. Who are the three highest catchers on the coast – yes, we are. Evens, we beat every crew that ever dived for perlemoen. But now they laugh at us. They choose the grounds and they take up twice what we do for half the work. They have machines and pumps and air-pipes and . . . Shut up! I'm talking. Get this right, fishing – finished!' He made a sweep with the flat of his hand. The two men looked at each other and back at Kleinhans. They both wore a white cloth tied over their hair and knotted at the back and old jeans rolled up to the knee. Side by side they squatted on their haunches facing him, and he felt vile and desperate with them making those slight sighing sounds of sorrow or distress, or whatever it was, and Stonewall dropping his eyes if he caught a straight stare. 'Finished!' He raised his voice and then half grumbled to himself, letting a handful of sand run through his fingers. 'I'll do what I damn well like, and they are not having the grin on me. If they want to see me down and out they have got a long wait coming.'

He caught the puzzled frown – 'All right, Stonewall. I thought of you, and Jefferson. You see my hand. I would cut it off for you.'

Stonewall made a tongue click and shook his head uneasily.

'I can't take you with me, see. I mean, I go to Cape Town. I am going to school there again, to college. I'm not good enough for some people here. But I'll come back and have my master's ticket and I'll be in a boat too big to get into this god-damned harbour. There will be a place for you, Stonewall, and you, Jefferson, if you are still here. So I thought of you, I got you jobs where you get twice what

I can pay. You work for Mister Momsen, you work on *Malmok*.'

'Haa,' they murmured together.

'You start with Mister Momsen today. You don't hold your breath when you dive. You have a mask and air-pipes and you walk about on the sea bottom like you are herding cattle, and you reap the perlemoen off the rocks like Kafir-corn.' He tried to smile, raising his eyes. But they weren't smiling.

'Well, that's how it is. Finished, *klaar*. Take my kit out of Swart's boat and put it back in the shed. One more thing. I owe you for the week. Here's a pound each. The rest I pay before I go.' He put the two blue-green notes on the hot white sand and a wind eddy from back of the wreck fluttered them. 'Well, what are you waiting for, man? It's your money, why don't you take it? Stonewall, pick it up before the wind blows it away.'

The little man shook his head, standing up in one clean movement. He was wringing his hands together. He wanted to reach out and touch the white man. Kleinhans looked up and saw his eyes were wet. 'Damn,' his lips framed, silent. 'Damn, damn!'

'Bwana, we do what you tell.'

Kleinhans did not look at him again. He heard the men's bare feet go off in the sand. The wind lifted the notes and blew them against his velskoen and then skidded them along the beach. 'God, they did it!' He rolled over on his face again. 'They left that bloody trash.'

He lay without moving a long time, a dark red emptiness under his closed eyelids. He wanted to sleep or to get up and run away and hide himself. It was not cold there; the sun, getting lower, still struck gratefully on him and only now and again the wind nagged around in eddies sprinkling him all over with fine sand. He could not stop thinking of the *Malmok* out in the harbour tugging gently at her moorings and the men getting ready, Stonewall and Jefferson among them. If he were skipper he would go out on the evening tide and be ready over the best perlemoen reefs when the light came and the sea motionless like ice and no wind. Stonewall and Jefferson dived without any kit beyond an eye-mask, a long tough-bladed knife and a net. Deeper than four or five fathoms he got them to take reserve bottles of air, but they preferred coming up like seals for a breather and they had never worked with air-pipes. They were like eels in the water, fast and agile, and when he or some of the other divers, with all their rubber skin-suits and jerseys, were blue and teeth chattering with cold, Stonewall and Jefferson were ready for another dive.

Kleinhans had gone down once close in to the reefs on a treacherous spring day with nearly an hour's supply of air. A lot can happen in an hour. He knew where the *Malmok* was anchored and could reach it in minutes. The rocks were clustered so thick with full-sized perlemoen, the shell-fish seemed almost jammed together. He would need a few minutes at the most to fill his net. Beyond him, the reef fell away into an under-sea canyon so deep he could not see bottom. But looming down there was something which looked like a ship's wreckage. He had left his net with its line and red marker-buoy and swum down to have a closer view. It was a wreck all right, of a big steel ship not more than thirty-odd years old. He hadn't heard of it before, and he thought of going on to explore, maybe find its name and poke into its holds for imperishable cargo – zinc or tin or lead that would bring him enough in salvage to pay off the

Malmok and keep him at college. He had a good look around. He could make out the name *Phalarion*, but all he found was bunker coal. He was surprised when he next checked on his watch – the hour had nearly gone. He could not find his net and he reckoned they had pulled it up. So he surfaced. And coming to the top was one of his biggest shocks. A tearing wind had sprung up and the sea had gone wild. His air-bottles were almost empty, and bobbing around on the broken swell he could get quite a range of vision as he topped the crests. First and foremost, there was no sign of *Malmok*. Sure, nobody but a madman would have risked her on the reef when the squall rose. He understood that. The crew had done the right thing and there was no hope of being picked up by *Malmok*. As for the dinghy – well, a dinghy could not make this sea or come out against the wind. He was a mile from land and that was his only hope, to swim ashore and trust on hitting a beach or cove and not the bare rock. He did not think much of his chances, but he struck out. He had been going twenty minutes and heard a shout. And there coming up behind him was the dinghy. It was doing the maddest things in the gale and alone in it like a wizard keeping it afloat by something more than human power was Stonewall. He never made out how Stonewall got him into the boat and kept it from being swamped. He was nearly dead with cold. Of course they could not turn back and Stonewall rowed down the wind, straight for the rocky coast. Kleinhans was steering and Stonewall shot the little craft between two blinders and across the surf-line. The dinghy was wrecked, but Stonewall got him ashore.

Afterwards he had a kind of shame about losing the boat, and on a trip making for the West Coast he squared his account. *Malmok* had her new dinghy in tow as usual, rounding the Cape, when they ran into the foulest Atlantic rollers. The dinghy was trying to leap clear off the water. And then the tow-line parted and it was good-bye to No. 2 boat. Kleinhans knew it to be death to get *Malmok* across the trough of the rollers and there was no circling to pick up the boat. He put the engine into reverse gear and slowed down, and then glancing back he saw the black naked body of Stonewall dive over the stern. Without a word he had gone into the icy Atlantic current and he was swimming like a seal. He got the tow-line of the dinghy in his teeth and began trying to swim back. It was too heavy for him to make much way, but *Malmok* was able to reverse, pick up the tow-line and Stonewall and keep her bow into the swell. When he got the boat tied secure and the trawler moving ahead again he called Stonewall and knocked him down backwards with a stunning crack over the eye. 'No boat is worth a man's life,' he said, helping Stonewall up. 'Remember that, you black donner.' Stonewall rubbed his face and grinned ruefully.

That night as he steered north leaving the lights of Cape Town far behind he heard the Nyasas singing a new song. He knew it was the song of the dinghy, or of the two dinghies. Gaily it sounded and he figured in it somewhere. Once he had got them to teach him a Nyasa song. It was about a girl whose man died. She went to the river and called out the two-headed water-snake, and it said she could have her man back if she gave it her baby. That was an old, old song with long, sad harmonics in which the singers interwove their voices in a difficult way. His two coloured crewmen thought it a bit strange for a white man to sing Kafir songs. But what would any other white man have thought –

'Kleinhans van As has not got all the calves in his kraal.'
Meaning he was daft. He did not care what they thought.

He lay in the sand and the afternoon was getting thin and
cold. Someone came by and halted there.

'Hello, Kleinhans,' a voice said. He recognised it was
Willie Momsen, but he did not stir a muscle. 'I thought I
would just say thanks for those two Nyasas of yours.' Still
he did not move. 'I'm going out tonight,' Willie said. 'Be on
the fishing-grounds daylight, at low tide.'

Momsen went off after that. He must have guessed
Kleinhans was awake. Maybe he also guessed how raw and
torn-up he was. Half an hour later Kleinhans heard the pom-
pom-pop! of the diesel motor start, levelling out into that
smooth, thrilling purr of pure unbridled power. He kept
his eyes closed. He could not bear to see *Malmok* go out,
steered down the tide by Willie Momsen.

During the night the Nyasas came out on deck and
squatted together with their backs to the galley house. The
wind had died and the only stir was the passing of the vessel.
The water was black glass and the moon, nearly full, climbing in the sky astern. Stonewall and Jefferson began singing.
They did not discuss it, but their hearts were in unison as
they made up a new song. Stonewall took the recitative and
his 'brother' harmonised or sometimes came in under Stonewall's higher tone with a vibrant hum. The song was
about Willie Momsen. It had a detailed description of his
parentage, his father's lack of liver and his mother's
abnormal organs and unnatural activities. Out of this union
sprang Willie, who, besides other things, was a herma-
phrodite and had six toes on each foot. His yard was a
dangling hag-fish, his heart a wallet crammed with pound

notes and his scrotum was stuffed with half-crowns that rattled and chinked dismally as he walked.

Momsen came up from the cabin and stood talking to the man at the wheel.

'It was a stroke of luck getting Kleinhans's Nyasas.'

'It was.'

'They are the best on the coast.'

'No doubt – I seen them at it.'

'Listen to them singing.'

'Ja, I been listening.'

'Kind of beautiful, eh?' Momsen said after a bit, calm, and drawing on his pipe.

'Ja, pretty nice. Considering they are Kafirs.'

'Well, that's why they sing. They are a happy-go-lucky lot.'

'Sure, the sods don't think much.'

'I wouldn't say that. It's far from home for them. Nyasaland – that's hell'n gone. A night like this. Well, it's . . . it's strange. It's sort of heart-rending, the little black fellows here out of their element and without a note of music or anything, and they can put up a show like that. Take a Gamatjie – unless he has a bottle of drink and a guitar he can't grind out a squeak.'

'That's right.'

'Or one of us. What do you sing when you're stone cold sober?'

'Me? Nothing.'

'And when you're drunk?'

'Damned if I know.'

'But listen to those two, they've really got something. They make me feel like a kid.' Momsen went aft and looked out at the Quoin lighthouse flashing away on the horizon.

The course was correct and the boat running at half speed. The moon-path lay along the black water.

Next day, as soon as the sun was high enough to strike into the water, they began diving. It was shallow water and so Stonewall and Jefferson went down without air. Momsen looked after the compressor and he watched the other men, but specially the Nyasas, active as eels. If they came up at the same moment and saw each other they would flash out a brilliant smile; a word and a laugh rippled over the still green water. It was so clear he could watch the divers at work on the bottom and see the fish cruising around them, unscared and curious as cats, waiting to pounce on any torn fragment from the perlemoen. The coloured boatman in the dinghy was kept busy hauling up the nets from the bright-painted marker buoys and the lockers of the divers were filling with shell-fish. The Nyasas were well out ahead with four or five hundred each before the midday break. Momsen had his rubber skin-suit on deck and he went down twice during the morning to relieve the white divers and give them a chance to thaw out in the sun. The water was cold, just on 50 F.

By lunch they had cleared most of the rocks of shell-fish above the legal size, and when Momsen moved out into deeper water to start again it meant everybody using air-pipes. Stonewall and Jefferson were more alarmed about the apparatus, the pipes and new-type masks, than about the sea or sharks or the tangling kelp. Momsen helped adjust their masks and belted on the air-valve cock at their sides. He explained how you turned the air supply on or off with your right hand, and he sent them down for short practice dives to get used to the kit. Then they took their nets and knives and made their first real dive. Momsen watched the

pipes and pressure dials carefully. He was a little anxious
about the Nyasas. Their courage and their cheerfulness were
impressive and he did not want any accidents. Soon he saw
something was wrong with Stonewall's air supply; the pipe
was jerking and the pressure built up. Stonewall was not
getting any air, and the depth was six or seven fathoms.
Bubbles were rising – that must be from the other men.
He had decided quickly to pull in Stonewall on the air-pipe,
and there suddenly about fifty feet away the little Nyasa
burst to the surface. He had wrenched off his air-mask and
came up bare-headed, made a great gasp and sank again.
By this time Momsen was paying in the air-pipe hand over
hand. Everything else was calm and still and there was no
sign of danger or death except the skipper feverishly hauling in Stonewall on the bright red pipe-line. The heavy
diving kit was keeping him down, but he was coming in
by yards a second. Momsen could see him now through the
green water, a big dark object. The pipe was attached to his
waist, but he was gripping it with his hands too. Momsen
got him alongside, and first his hands then his head came
up into the air. He was alive all right, he moved his head
and a gush of water came out of his mouth. There was only
six feet to go to have Stonewall over the boat's side on
deck, and Momsen crazily began hoisting him on the pipe.
As he came up out of the water the weight increased.
Momsen was a powerful man and to him the ten stone of
the fisherman and his kit was a lightweight. Stonewall was
hanging clear of the water when the pipe snapped and
slipped through his convulsively clutching hands and he
fell back like a rock. He went straight down. Momsen was
a strong swimmer, but he did not dive at once after Stonewall. First he shouted to the boatman to come alongside

and take over the watch. He grabbed his skin-suit and started climbing into it, and he pulled on his frog-feet, strapped his helmet and mask and checked the air compression. Say that took him five minutes. He was ready, but he was five minutes too late. He went over with a splash and dived. The two white divers had surfaced and they were amazed seeing him disappear and leave the *Malmok* to herself. The boatman was not yet on deck. Momsen found Stonewall on the sea floor and brought him up. They all helped lift him on deck and worked on him. But he was dead.

On the way back to harbour they gave Stonewall's body into his brother's care and the Nyasa did not say anything. He did not cry or complain. He knew what had happened and his silence added to Momsen's feeling of wretchedness. Jefferson got a spike and string and he folded his brother up close, the shape he was when he lay in the womb, and sewed him in a blanket. The *Malmok* returned at full speed and and that was what they brought ashore in the dinghy about ten o'clock the same night, a bundle sewn up in a red blanket.

Alida had come down, seeing light on *Malmok*'s moorings out in the harbour basin, and she got to the jetty just after they had landed Stonewall's body. Jefferson was standing silent near the shape. Momsen told her what had happened. 'I believe he bumped the air-valve cock with his elbow. Any diver knows how to turn the air on again. He knew, I showed him myself, but he must have panicked – yes, he panicked.' Alida sensed by his manner there was something more he had not told her, she guessed his cowardice and his hand in the fisherman's death. He drove her home to her father's house and after he had gone off to report to the police Alida walked down the single village street to the Imperial Hotel, a one-storey iron-roof canteen. She went in the lounge and sent the night watchman through to the bar to call Kleinhans van As. There was a big noise going on in the bar and she wondered if Kleinhans was there or if he had been beaten up and thrown out hours before. The door from the bar opened with a burst of noise and there was Kleinhans. He stood for fully a minute and then turned and slammed the door in the faces of the men clustering behind him to stare. He came across and tried to bow.

'Mejuffrou Wessels,' he said. She felt sick at his red puffed face and bloodshot eyes and the thickness on his tongue that made his effort at sarcasm disgusting.

'Kleinhans, try and listen to what I say.'

'But – nach – 'rally . . .'

'Be quiet and listen. Your man Stonewall is dead. They killed him diving at sea. . . . Be quiet and let me finish. . . .' She told him exactly to the word what Momsen had said and added nothing. He had fallen into a chair and his face had gone deadly white. Long after she had stopped he still sat there, staring downwards and gripping the table edge.

'Do you understand what I have said, Kleinhans?'

'Thank you, Alida. Leave . . . this to me.'

By the time Kleinhans reached the harbour the jetty was deserted. The village had turned in to sleep. The power plant had been shut off for the night and beyond a window here and there with a dim candle he could see no sign of anyone astir. Stonewall's body had been taken to the location a mile off and Momsen had gone to see the police in the district centre. In the moonlight Kleinhans could see *Malmok* out there like a silver gull asleep on the water. He walked down the shelving of the slipway, knelt between the boat-rails and cupped up water to splash in his face. The lap of a slow swell wet his knees. He did not move away. And then, without knowing it, he was sobbing. He put down his hands for support in the shallow water and hung his head and the sobs shook down his spine, stabbing him with pain and horror and shame. Another small wave lapped at him and another before he struggled to his feet. He felt sober, cold and ill. He went to Swart's boat-shed and took out his frog-feet and a steel crowbar and then he stripped and waded down into the chilling water. It made him gasp and draw heavy breath. Getting across the stretch of open water and keeping afloat with the weight of the bar was utter hell. His heart was near bursting and he never would make it; he thought of dropping the bar and giving over his plan. Or he would go down with it, he had only to hold on to the weight of it and stop struggling. *Malmok* seemed miles off. Then his head scraped on the mooring cable, and he reached out and took a hold on it. He got up and on to the deck and for a long while, swinging away into moments of half-consciousness, he lay on the planks recovering his strength. Then he stood up and smoothed his wet hair back off his face and went to work in the bright clear moonlight with the crowbar. He started on the compressor, smashing at it methodically. It was not a difficult thing to wreck – he burst the castings and got the steel point in and wrenched and tore at it. As he worked, his body warmed up and a berserker madness swarmed as a black cloud over his brain. He rushed at the deck-house and smashed the heavy glass. Everything inside he drove at wildly; he shattered the compass and wheel and radio set. Momsen had installed an echo-sounding device to locate deep-sea shoals and he shoved the bar through it with one blow. It was quite light in the deck-house but down below in the engine-room he had to grope about, knowing his whereabouts from memory. Now he was killing the little ship itself. He crashed and levered at the diesel motor, grunting as he felt the metalwork give. The injectors and water housing and camshaft assembly snapped and cracked as he wrenched at them. And at last the moment had come that he had been putting off through all the orgy of destruction. He was going to scuttle the ship. He raised the crowbar, sharp point downwards, and brought it with a thump against the bottom timber. Once, twice. He stopped and felt with his fingers at the deep four-sided holes he had made in the wood. No water was coming in. It was like feeling at the wounds of a living thing. *Malmok*, he thought, his own boat. He had done his worst and he could not sink her, he could not murder her. What in hell had he been doing? But not that. The last thing would live within him for ever as a black sin, the foulest thing he ever did. Momsen had killed Stonewall, of that he was certain, and now he had avenged the little Nyasa. He could not add to it the sinking of the beautiful *Malmok*. That was not in any call between man and man.

Kleinhans went up on deck and dropped the crowbar without a sound or a splash into the water. He dragged on his frog-feet and swam ashore. One thing he had done – he had saved the boat *Malmok*, but he had saved it from himself. He had given Stonewall's life away to Momsen and now he had given away the right ever to regain the fishing-boat. He had to start again somewhere else.

The first to go aboard *Malmok* the day following was Jefferson, taking a line from the dinghy carrying her crew. Momsen had offered him time off but he had refused and brought another Nyasa to fill Stonewall's place. He stood on the deck staring, and the others had to tie up and come crowding after him. He walked about, peering at the wreckage with a strange air of certainty. He was not surprised. Momsen noticed it and the others noticed too. He even smiled.

'What's this, Jefferson——' Momsen came up to him – 'Did you know it had been done?'

'No, Bwana.'

'What are you so happy about then, damn it?'

'Bwana, Stonewall, his spook been here. He done all smash-up.'

'Oh, for Christ's sake.'

'Stonewall spook come back night-time. He leave ship. Bwana Kleinhans, his ship.'

The Nyasas buried Stonewall in the bush beyond the location, sitting in his grave facing the west inside the red blanket and with a knife and an assegai and some plates of food. They lit a fire and beat on empty oil drums and the people of other races and tribes stood around in the ring of firelight, watching. Jefferson was not downcast and Kleinhans looked at him with pain and absolute bewilderment. And when they spoke, Jefferson told him Stonewall's ghost had come back and smashed up *Malmok*. The ghost was free now and would return home with his blankets and personal things, home to Nyasaland.

'Jefferson, I did it. I smashed up *Malmok*.'

'No, Bwana – Stonewall – him do it.'

'I tell you I swam out there and I bust up the boat myself.'

Jefferson smiled and bent his head respectfully, but he had a knowing look in his eyes.

'You and Stonewall, Bwana. You help him.'

'Don't touch me, don't touch me. You will regret it.'

He took her by the jaw with one hand and his fingers pressed into the soft flesh of her cheek and throat. Seeing her so close under the light, he turned paler. The wild, bitter rage, the unquenched hate in her look gave him a start of physical fear.

'Are you mad?' he said in his old private voice. And then in the voice and manner which had slowly taken possession of him he began to shout in her face. His colour came back. He was the public man, the country auctioneer, loud, brash.

'What can you do, threatening me?'

'Leave me alone,' she said, and she repeated in a way that chilled him. 'You will regret it, when you are sober.'

'What have I to regret, what more, tell me that. Hell! And why don't you tell me whose child you are carrying?'

She shook off his hand and panting for breath in a way that sounded like a succession of little sighs she said, looking him in the eyes: 'Danie, before my Holy Maker I have never dishonoured you, all the time I have been alone – never. Ah, but what you have done to me . . .'

'Take that back. It's a lie!'

'I will not take back one word and I have not . . .'

He struck her in the face and she stumbled against the table. She turned and he struck her again, shouting in her face.

'Ah, ah,' she panted. She went through to the bedroom and

while he poured a drink he heard her moving about. He went out on the stoep and at first it was totally dark and the fine rain trickled in the down-pipes. But it was a luminous night with a moon somewhere behind the clouds and he could make out the big bulk of the trees standing quite motionless and dripping. The town was two miles off and the nearest house was the forest station on the hill-top beyond the road. The light shone across the garden from the bedroom window on the white trunk of a tree. Her shadow moved across the light once, twice. He was alarmed again, remembering her expression, the insane concentration that told him as nothing else could the utter truth in her heart. She, small and alone, had the unbearable power to make him afraid.

He heard her footstep on the threshold and she came out on the stoep. She had put on a light raincoat and on one arm was their two-and-a-half-year-old Grieta wrapped in a blanket and a black shawl. In her free hand she carried a small suitcase.

'So!' he put down his glass on the stoep wall.

'Good-bye, you will never see me again.'

'So you want to shame me.'

She merely fixed on him her dark, large eyes.

'You are running away, you are a coward, Johanna.'

'I am no coward.' She shuddered and her lips trembled so violently that he suddenly laughed.

'Go on, go on then! And where are you heading?'

'I should tell you.'

'All right – and you will be back in half an hour. There's nothing out there but the darkness and the forest. And between here and the town no one at all, only the bush Kafirs and the Kafirs in the cutters' camp. A nice lot. How will you get past them?'

194

She went down the steps terribly afraid he would stop her. Her one thought was to get past him and she dared not say anything in case his mood changed and he came down after her. Grieta was asleep and her head rested on her shoulder.

She walked quickly and came out of the open gate on the road. It was all quiet and muffled under the fine soft drizzle; no sound save the drip from the trees and an occasional rustle going through the leaves like a breath. In her anxiety to get free from the house she had almost run, pausing in moments to listen for her husband's footsteps, and then hurrying on. She did not notice the weight of Grieta or of the case. Being six months with her second baby she did not have her old strength and was easily tired. He had called her mad. Perhaps she was mad. She did not feel things as she used to – she was not fine and balanced and sensitive to all things at once as a girl was, but her mind swung about clumsily like a heavy weather-vane. At one moment she was full of a raging self-pity. And then fear took her, fear of all sorts of unknown things, fear for Grieta and herself and the unborn baby, nightmares of fear. And another mood that shut out all other feelings was remorse, bitter regret for the past, for her failings, her love of Danie that she could not keep alive.

They were building two houses on speculation down the road from their entrance and she could smell the wet timber and cement. Nobody would be there, not even a watchman. She stood in the road, thinking. Towards the town was the cutters' camp. She was frightened of the hard, fierce men living there, black men who were part of the night, wandering the road in ones and twos. The twin thoughts of night on the endless veld and of its possessor the black man were, in her generations, a deep blood-anxiety. Sometimes looking at the dark window-panes when her husband was away for the country auctions she would see gleaming eyes in a black face. It might be her face in the glass or a wild fancy, but it made her heart stop.

Then she thought her husband, if he followed her in the car, would overtake her on the road to the town. That decided her. She turned the other way thinking to spend the night at the forest station. Geldenhuys, the sub-forester, was an uncouth man, often drunk, but his wife would take in any soul, out of pity. They had twelve children.

She had to keep on the alert for the forest road, a mere gap in the dark wall of trees, and once she went back a little way, thinking she had passed it by. But she found it and heard the water gurgling under the cross-culvert. It was from now on a mere track through the wood and plantations, two paths beaten by truck tyres and grown between with bracken and tough grass and a weed that gave up a strong wild scent when trodden on. Above was the faint ribbon of the sky and sometimes she passed clearings dotted with pale stumps and timber piles.

Now her whole mind swung on the thought of reaching the Geldenhuys cottage. She was not afraid or anxious, but over her limbs and muscles and joints was settling a lead blanket of weariness. She thought how far she had come and how much farther to go. She must be half-way – no, not nearly that. The weight of Grieta was drawing fiery bands of fatigue under her shoulder-blades and she set down the case more frequently how to change the child from one arm to the other. If only she could sling her on her back in a blanket like a Kafir woman. But that was a custom, and she would not be seen doing it. Who would see her, there, at night? All the while the road was climbing but dipped sometimes into a gully and the water of a stream talked to her quietly in its culvert. The rain was slowly soaking the shawl and blanket round Grieta – how the child slept! Heart against heart, and the little one fearing nothing.

She stopped to change Grieta again. The forest was thick and close on all sides and the tree-tops almost touching above. So dark she could hardly see to arrange the folds of the blanket. The child woke and began whimpering.

'Sshh darling, Mammie is holding you,' she crooned. She rocked the big wet bundle and her heart was low; she wanted to sit on the ground and cry. Could she ever get to the cottage? And what if she had taken a wrong turning of the service track. It wound here and there and she could not remember if there were forks or crossings.

At last the child fell asleep again. She settled its weight on her hip and bent to pick up the case. Away off in the darkness she heard the sound of plucked strings. She listened. Five or six falling notes, ending on a low, distinct beat. The hair seemed to rise on the back of her neck and a feeling of numb cold entered her hands and around her lips. The notes were repeated, varied, soft and faint guitar notes always ending on the same beat – toom –toom! From the first moment she knew beyond doubt what it was, it was the way a Kafir played a guitar. He walked through the night playing, it was his private music played to himself, his private night. A man playing music might not be dangerous, but how could one tell? It was his way of proclaiming himself, his contempt of everything, his possession of the darkness. Toom – toom, the low note repeating.

She wanted to turn and run, but which way? The sound of the guitar came out of the night as if it were a ripple on the forest's slow soft breath. It was everywhere, now a clear note and now an echo among the dripping trees. She stood so deathly still that Grieta woke again and began talking in a sleepy, milk-warm voice.

'Why is it so dark? Where are we, Mammie?'

'Sshh, my baby-lamb. Go to sleep again. We are going to see Oom Flip and them.'

'Why are you whispering, Mammie?'

'Sshh, lamb.' They both listened to the guitar.

'Who is that playing, is it Oom Flip?'

The mother kissed her. 'It might be. Are you quite warm, my love?'

'I'm so warm! But your face is wet, Mammie, are you crying? Look! there's a light.'

There was a flare of a match being lit off to the left and for a moment it shone like a spark at the end of a long tunnel. It went out. The guitar had stopped and now she heard voices, liquid voices of the black people, and one laughed. They were ahead of her and coming down the track. If she ran now she could escape them; tired as she was she could run home. But she did not move. Her heart and stomach were going in strange, painful flutters and the ground heaved dizzily.

She let the case slip to the ground and sank down on it, folding Grieta in both her arms. 'Lord save me, Lord save this child of mine.' She felt firmer and her head cleared and she was busy for a minute making Grieta comfortable on her lap. It was no use running. She had no strength and nowhere to go. Not back to her husband.

The men's footsteps were quite plain to hear now. She could see nothing but imagined them, one on each wheel-track swinging easily along and at home in the forest and the darkness. The night was theirs and she was in their hands. The guitar started again and Grieta, who had caught her terror, gripped her, crying.

The guitar stopped. They came up cautiously, there were two men looking huge looming shapes in their greatcoats, and one struck a match.

'Hai! hai!' he said intensely, 'a white *nooi*, and a child.'

The other, who was taller almost by a head, laughed in a strange, almost childish embarrassment, as if such an event were beyond him.

'Where is the *nooi* going?' the smaller man asked. She had seen by the flare of his match a glistening, savage face, the skin roughly pitted and eyes almost lost between high cheek-bones and a bony brow. And yet the voice was mild; it could not be the same man.

The mother tried to answer but no sound came from her. Grieta said: 'We are going to Oom Flip.'

'Ha!' they both murmured together.

'It is a long way,' the shorter man said. 'We will take you.'

'No,' the mother said, 'I will go by myself. I was only resting, I will go now.'

She stood up although her knees trembled. Her supreme moment, she knew, had come. She picked up the case and with all the authority and firmness left in her she said: 'Now, leave me.'

'Give me the case,' the smaller man said.

She relaxed her fingers and let it fall. 'Take it and leave me. Leave me and my child.'

He took the case and handed it to his companion. She began walking. Grieta clung to her, quiet and tense and her eyes round like a little bush-baby. The men followed. She knew they were behind her and she did not know how long she could go on without screaming. No one would hear, and a scream might rouse them. They whispered to each other. She went on and on, she could not stop now. Grieta's head sank against her breast and she fell asleep. It was a miracle, she thought, that the child could sleep. 'Lord save her. Lord save us,' she repeated under her breath. The track dipped fairly steeply to cross a gully and there was an opening in the trees to the right, the sky lifting and full of suffused moonlight. The weight of the child made a burning stripe of pain over her shoulders and it was impossible, going downhill, to keep her knees and ankles from wobbling. She turned her shoe on a loose stone and stumbled but still kept Grieta in her arms. In a moment the black man caught up with her. 'Give me the child, *nooi*,' he said. He took the sleeping baby in her bundle, opened one side of his greatcoat and made a big pouch for her. She disappeared into the coat. He had an acrid smell of wood-smoke and tobacco and sweat. The child went on sleeping in the warm shelter against the smell and the movement of his iron-hard body.

He went ahead and the mother followed, and behind them came the tall man carrying the bag. The guitar was slung by a string on the leader's back and it was a silent procession until he began to sing. She did not understand the words but the song was sad and gentle. It had the melancholy of the guitar music yet it was more complicated, falling in slow rhythms. The man behind added his deeper voice in a natural harmonic and the two seemed to share a feeling between them that shut out and excluded her utterly. Still, she was carried along between them and her limbs were like machines and the dead weight of fatigue slipped off her. In her heart was a small flame of gladness and a sense of safety.

Grieta was safe. In the strong, bitter-smelling folds of the man's coat she was secure. She could not have come all this way without them, she would have fallen and lain there and maybe miscarried. How terrified she had been.

At the forest station a dog barked at them, a small white dog that darted among their legs and almost choked in the fierceness of its alarm. The taller man went on the stoep and banged at the door. 'Baas, baas, baas Flip!'

They banged again and called. Suddenly the door was wrenched open and a tall whiteman stood on the threshold with a rifle in one hand and carrying a storm lantern. 'Ja?'

He was in a crumpled shirt and khaki trousers and locks of unkempt grey hair straggled down to his beard.

'Baas, we found the *nooi* in the forest and brought her to you.'

He looked at them in turn, holding up the light. 'Mevrou,' he said, astounded, 'Mevrou, what is the meaning of this?'

'Let me rest,' she said. She took Grieta from the man. 'Thank you,' she said.

'Now clear off,' the forester shouted. 'Ah, you vagabonds. Don't let me catch you in these forests.'

'Baas Flip, what have we done?'

'Don't ask me, but you are up to no good. That I know.'

They grinned and touched their hats and together they faded back into the darkness. The forester went in to drag his wife from her bed and the mother could hear her sleepy voice somewhere inside the dim, close-smelling house. With all those children sleeping two and three in a bed she knew there would be no place for her, but she sat on a box on the stoep too tired to care. The rain had stopped and somewhere down in the forest the guitar began its endless little private tune coming always to the deep beat, toom – toom. It did not disturb her. Grieta was sleeping and the bundle in which she was wrapped still had the smoky acrid smell of the man. Listening and half drowsing she felt mysteriously safe.

THREE WOMEN

The second day they met as woman to woman. Two people, strangers divided by uncharted and bleak spaces brought suddenly so near they might hear each other's heartbeat. The first meeting at the hall had been stuffed with formalities, surrounded by all the committee members and functionaries and well-wishers. Now they met at close quarters, on guard, wary and sensitive.

The new medical superintendent, Dr Magdalena du Plessis, had come into the small District Hospital precisely at eight o'clock for her morning round. Everyone in the humdrum level of the hospital's daily work was ready to size her up, the patients and staff, and the floor-scrubber who had finished his task an hour before, and even the gay little club-foot gardener. They were all Zulus, sharp in their manner of scrutinising a stranger under shaded lashes. What they took in of Magdalena made them pause and a quiver went through them as if a thin mist shadow had passed over the sun and as suddenly vanished. They noted with the sureness of instinct the undaunted look in her eyes, blue eyes, alive and full of fire, blue of a flame that startles you in the heart of a fire, or of frost by moonlight. They felt uncomfortable.

Before they had seen her she had been something general and average in their conversation – the Boer Woman. Just as 'Government' was a little sunless man in the enormous heart of a concrete building, so 'Government' was sending

them an amorphous Boer Woman to take over from the re-
tiring English doctor. They had called him 'Weaver-bird' for
his eyebrows were so shaggy a finch could build its nest in
them. A tangible man – one could feel him, savour his weakness and cast him into tale or jibe. Now a living spark in the
sky-coloured eyes of the new doctor at once shattered that
muffling vagueness of the picture they had formed, making
them uneasy. They did not much note that she was small
and pale and exquisitely neat in her white uniform, her
hands slender and long-fingered and a slight smile touching
her mouth that was disarming but also disconcerting.

Dr Magdalena du Plessis entered the female ward and
there they met. The other woman was her chief assistant in
the District Hospital, Sister Scholastica.

The sister stepped lightly down the ward aisle smiling
brilliantly and they exchanged a brisk though friendly greeting. Beside her superior, the Zulu woman was gorgeous in
every way, sumptuous. She was young, or rather ageless,
big and full-figured and a high bloom on her dark chocolate
skin, large bold eyes centring to glittering blackness and
her teeth incomparably pure and white.

'Is there anything exceptional?' the doctor asked.

'Nothing but the exceptional cold,' Sister Scholastica
laughed. 'The pipes are still frozen.'

'And no water in the kitchen?'

'Only hot from the cylinder, but we should have the
supply through in half an hour.'

The doctor studied the report sheet, glancing at the black
faces of the patients against the white of their pillows. All
were tense but mute, steeled by endurance against pain and
the patience of their race. All watched her like two rows of
gargoyles but as they met the steely, impersonal glance of

their new doctor they were confused. No longer the Boer Woman – they would call her One who Watches from Beyond the Fire. It would imply that they might never understand or admit her intimacy but beware of her.

She now took the west side and went easily from bed to bed followed by Sister Scholastica and two frightened young nurse-aids. The sun shone bright but thin across the ward, probing through curtainless windows with a pitiless light into every corner of the long, bleak and sad room. Sad with silent pain and endurance and the memories of death. The feel of the ward in a few moments shuddered on her senses and, as she went on, sent her heart down into numb deeps. The beds had been smartened up with clean coverlets, but under their hygienic surface was a different order of reality – of unwashed bodies, dirt and stench. She flipped back a corner and clenched her teeth. There were faked temperature charts too, obvious in a moment. Each card had been traced in to date with flourishing zigzags, as if the ritual were enough without the meaning. Dr du Plessis had heard before of this failing, been forewarned by the Provincial Medical chief, Dr Graham, but the impact had not then shaken her as it did now. What made it possible, and was a faked chart a deception or an illusion? She held down the outburst rising in her and stood a moment with one hand pressed on the forehead of an old woman sunk in a stupor of fever.

'We will come back to her,' she said, quiet but suppressed. Sister Scholastica made a pencil note. Her eyes were dilated and she could feel her own pulse drumming in her ears. She hoped the round would go off without an upheaval. And after that – well, after that the responsibility for everything in the hospital would fall on the white woman. Any failing, and one could always answer: 'But you did not tell me, you did not give orders, it is not in the hospital rules.'

She had assumed a self-soothing confidence that the new doctor might turn out as easy-going as old 'Weaver-bird'. He did not believe in mollycoddling the patients and treated them with what he called 'Kafir psychology' – large potions of bright-coloured liquid and an invariable hypodermic injection, even if only of sterile water. It was a misplaced hope. This little medico was not likely to be easy-going. She could see it in the slight quiver of her nostrils and chiefly in those eyes which could ring sharp blows. Strange that she said nothing. At the end of the row was a bed behind screens, the patient an old Indian woman, set apart from the Zulus by the barrier of race but more so by shadows sifting over her of death. She lay half exposed in filthy blankets; a spasm ran through her, wrenching up the sinews of her neck. Alone, she was fighting out the last unequal battle of a pinched life. Sister Scholastica quickly pulled up the disordered blankets, tucked down the coverlet and turned over the soiled pillow; lively in each movement, efficient, but dropping back the lolling grey head heartlessly.

'Everything possible has been done for her,' she said with professional detachment. 'But she is dying.'

There once more was the unreal zigzag of a temperature chart – an incantation to science – and less scientific, the putrid smell rising from the bed. In what seemed a lucid moment the woman steadied her gaze and stared gauntly up at the white doctor, moving her lips soundlessly.

'Terrible,' Magdalena whispered to herself.

She dismissed the sister and her two aids and walked back alone to the office. From the door she caught a last glance of the magnificent Zulu woman. She was handing out linen to the nurses, supple and balanced, smiling. Immaculate in every detail of her person, her veil crisp and snowy, brown shoes gleaming, dignity in the purple shoulder straps and a stiff white belt braced to the soundness and grace of her figure. Such a paragon could glide above mere trifles in the female ward. Where was the illusion and where the essence?

The office enclosed her again in the same bleakness and chill she had left behind in the ward, bare white walls, paper and rubbish in the fire-grate and an ink-stained desk with nothing on it but a dry crusted inkpot. Dr du Plessis put down the report sheet and sat staring through and past it. What to do – where to begin? She had the feeling this place was not true and her actions would become clogged down as in a dream. Her sense of order was violently affronted; if only she could turn the whole hospital upside down to let in breath and daylight. She would like to strip Sister Scholastica of her rank and see her start down on her knees again scrubbing and washing and cleaning. Scholastica! what a name, and what a façade. No, she was bound to deal gently with the staff, to know and understand and sympathise. Chief of all the resplendent sister. A difficult assignment, was what Dr Graham had said. 'You are not going to find things plain sailing and our future plans will depend on you, on your success with the place. It is not one of our bright spots. We want to rebuild, double or treble its capacity to take off some of the load on the central hospitals. A lot will depend on you.'

'Aren't you expecting too much from me, Dr Graham?' she had parried.

'No. We are asking a great deal, but not too much.'

Then he had pushed away his papers, clearing everything from the space between them and spoken to her directly but drily, thinking carefully. Through his words came a secret warmth, a fanaticism, and not for the mere practical success of his profession. She had glimpsed in him something of the zeal that went beyond a man's work and took on its own life.

'You speak the language, Magdalena, it is a great advantage but it does not mean you understand a Zulu. There's no pattern and there are no easy answers. There are no short cuts, for them or for us. I want you to remember this always in handling staff especially. We are short on everything, short on personnel, on training and short above all on quality. We can't afford to lose a nurse or let a single one slip back on her training. I will try to send you staff but you must keep them, help them along, raise their quality. And don't be impatient – in them we can see our own faults.

'Magdalena, we take unconsciously what has come to us over thousands of years, what a smart platform speaker calls civilisation. I'm not going to be smart, but dealing with your problem you must build on what exists and not on what you wish for. Only people are real; remember the qualities we have in common and build on them. You can say love is something shared by all humans, mother love and sexual love and family love. We can almost take them for granted, being born to them. Also love of life and the instinct of mutual defence in the herd. But some qualities we value are not natural. In fact they are so strange and contrary to the savage native instincts of a human that they can take root only at the cost of changing him utterly; they force him into new paths. By the same token, he can shed them at will and slip back into the old savagery. One of them is pity, and another is truth. They can never be taken for granted. We can be ruthless and we all lie, I mean in the darkest and most lamentable sense. It is a bit too easy to condemn a Zulu for being a bad whiteman. And difficult, maybe a bit too difficult for our generation, to wait and help him over. He will make the grade of course. But when? When will Euripides and Aristotle be an unconscious part of his soul? And likewise Jesus and Avicen, Augustine, Galen, Erasmus and Milton and Newton. . . ?'

She had looked at him with such an expression of amazement that he stopped and smiled wrily, abashed at having so ponderously lectured his young and pretty colleague. But he held to his point and repeated quietly: 'Pity and truth. You see what I mean?'

'I think I do,' she had replied and got up to leave.

She had not known whether to resent Dr Graham's homily. Of course he had meant her to be forbearing, patient to build up civilised standards, especially among her own staff. He saw the medical service in scientific terms but also as an outpost of the spirit. Still, she could not help feeling his words had been pointed also at her personally. He from his British standpoint was reminding her, an Afrikaner, of the greater things in their common lineage. Did he think her in danger of forgetting them? Truth and pity – had the British always remembered? Granted the barbarian was merciless and perfidious, Norsemen and Germani as much as Zulus and Matabele. But what of the civilised conqueror and the modern ruler? Dr Graham raised instead the personal issue; he referred this most sacred of human bonds to each one's inner conscience. He knew her well and had backed her through Medical School with a state scholarship. He had a right to use her Christian name. And now he had sent her to this terribly exacting assignment with a heavy charge, to remember her humanity more than her race, the greatness of past generations and not the narrowness of the present.

The new doctor brought changes into the wards by personal example. She sat all night through the crisis of the old fever-bitten woman; kept her warm against the frosty night, saw to the changing of a sweat-soaked shift, and by all the limited means available she exploited the flickering strength left in a worn frame. At alternate periods she sent the sister and nurses heavy-eyed to bed and stayed herself, feeling the pulse stagger on like a tired foot-traveller nearing home on the rim of some vast valley beyond which there was nothing.

She sometimes kept up a quiet run of talk, in Zulu but mostly in English, to tell the nurses exactly what she was doing, describing the patient's condition and its causes. And she was trying all the while to evoke a response, to stir them beyond what seemed a passive duty. Despite their presence her heart could not escape out of an infinite loneliness. When the response came it was unexpected. She had dismissed the youngest nurse-aid in the cold dark hour before dawn and suddenly the girl took her hand for an instant in both hers and squeezed it. A little gesture of tenderness or gratitude or love and she smiled, looking into the round black face and glistening eyes. Neither of them spoke.

The old woman lived and they said in the ward: 'She belongs to the doctor.' The Indian woman died. She had no relations. Nobody knew where she was born or where she had come from. But she died in a clean bed and the wife of a trader came in and burnt joss-stick incense near her as she lay peacefully near her end.

The patients were washed. Oil drums hammered into rough braziers were lit at sundown and carried to glow all night in the wards so the night nurse stayed on duty and was not perished with cold.

Sister Scholastica approved of the changes. She took much of the credit for them to herself and flounced about for a few days with an added air of authority. She scolded the junior staff for any lapse from doctor's orders. When she sold food from the hospital kitchen to her numerous hangers-on it was no longer slapped into filthy billy-cans and jam tins. The containers had to be hygienic, the bread wrapped. To the patients in the men's ward who habitually complained of being starved she now had the final withering answer. 'The doctor says so. If you eat more you will die – ask her yourself.' They were silent.

Magdalena's rounds of the wards were eagerly awaited and the men in particular, keen but friendly-eyed, watched for the first sign of a slip. They liked to draw her into a long-winded discussion on some trivial point and smiled at the sharpness of her wisdom or her use of the language. Such a woman was beyond description, her spirit like a flying blade and an understanding unmeasured as a pool in which lived the two-headed snake. In her presence they made no complaint and sweated out their pain in silence. Better death than the weakness of a groan. If they saw at her side the open book of Sister Scholastica's smiling face they did not betray their thoughts.

The sister knew in her heart it could not last. No human being, let alone a slim small woman, could stand the pace set by the doctor. She would be up most of the night and start again at dawn. All afternoon she attended to the hundreds of out-patients who streamed to her clinic. Her régime of washing was wearing out the staff and driving the patients to despair; her discipline had everybody on edge. The sheer rigour and mystery of her sudden success began to attract patients from beyond the radius of the District Hospital. Each morning except Sundays they would be huddled in their greasy blankets on the stoep to see the One who Watches from Beyond the Fire.

The more she attempted the more they overwhelmed her. The staff resigned their will and initiative and their very thoughts to her. There was no longer the need for them to remember anything since she was the final repository of all knowledge. She refused to concede to primordial custom by even a pretence of divining sickness. New patients expected a doctor, whether white or black, to know their ills by magical incantation, so that when Magdalena asked bluntly what was the matter they lied and twisted, giving her the double task of penetrating the disguise and then of laying open the true symptoms.

Sister Scholastica was grateful, she was lost in admiration for her new superior whom she at once raised as an idol, bringing her an adoration touched with awe. She could not imagine how the hospital had carried on without her. The club-foot gardener would come grinning to the kitchen door to ask whether he must water the peas or plant carrots and her brain did not register the question.

'Go and ask the doctor,' was her reply before the words were out. In the days of old 'Weaver-bird' she had tyrannised patients with the threat of having them washed in cold water; under the new régime her attitude underwent a revolution and now she made it a special favour to let a patient off a washing. Inside of a week she had subsided again with barely a jolt into a tolerable though subtly changed complacency. Punctual, immaculate and splendid as ever, still a larger glow seemed to radiate from her pride in a task beautifully done.

The hard irksome details crammed into her head during training had long since grown blurred, rubbed down in memory, but she remained intuitively practical through routine and was capable of rising calmly to an emergency. All she need do then was to watch the doctor. And if the doctor were not present, who was any the worse or the wiser if she did nothing?

The sister lay in bed on a Saturday night comfortably relaxed in mind and body. The hospital slipped out of her thoughts, the crowded wards, patients on mattresses between the beds. Sleep was sliding sensuously upon her. Outside, a bitter dry wind blew unseen dust across the veld, nagged at shacks in the location. It came to her as the breathing of some great sprawling creature. The man lying at her side kept talking to her in a soft, far-away voice.

'. . . and when they are gone we will be happy. In our own land.'

'Ah——' came from her dreamily – 'happy.'

'Haayi . . . no more shouting, no swearing. Jim, come here! Hey, you, Kafir! No more . . . fetch this, pick up that, bloody bastard . . .'

'Aha.'

'Drive our own trains, and make them travel third class. Run our hospitals . . . make them scrub floors.'

She smiled in the dark. Let him talk, poor boy, what did he know? Who would choose to run a hospital? She didn't scrub floors and she didn't want to run the place. Never. Not for him or anyone else. She turned over and pushed him unwittingly but firmly to the very edge of the bed. The cold air crept up, yet he lay and waited for her to roll back and give him more room.

'A man must be a man, his own boss,' the warm silken voice went on. 'They won't call us "boy", not in our own land. Boy, make the tea! Boy . . . boy . . . damn you, boy! If they don't like it let them clear out. . . . What do you say?' He nudged her with his elbow. Her senses had lapsed finally into sleep but the strong supple body heaved back against his pressure and he tumbled hard on the floor-boards. He lay there dazed a moment, cursing. Then he realised someone was knocking insistently, louder and louder, at the door. In a panic he slid under the bed and lay still. What if it were the doctor? It was cold but he lay quite motionless and listened to the knocking. How long would it take to wake her? He heaved with his knees under the bed-springs and heard her grunt; once again, she was awake.

'Yes, what is it?'

'A patient, Sister, crying to come in.'

'Tell him to come Monday.'

'It is a woman. I told her, but she keeps crying to come in.'

'What! At this time of the night – who does she think she is?'

'Sister, the woman will not listen.'

She was out of bed and he heard her thump across the floor. The lock rattled; a shaft of light slashed the room. Then he glimpsed her as she swept out drawing a wrap round her with an angry gesture. She had forgotten about him there under the bed, snapped him contemptuously out of her mind and gone back in wrath to her world where she was a figure of awe and mastery and he would not dare

214

follow her. He was glad, he thought, climbing back in bed, glad in his heart he was not the woman crying at the door.

Sister Scholastica brushed quickly through the female ward. To the patient who was awake and saw her pass she looked larger than life in her thick white wrap as a figure seen through mist. She had regained her balance and her slippered footfalls made little sound. She was angry. People knew who she was and they should know better than to beat at the entrance and upset the whole hospital after midnight. She strode through the lobby and swung back the main door.

The third woman sat there on the concrete in the meek pose dictated by custom, and yet there was something awkward and repellent about her. So close that she could sway forward and tap-tap-tap at the panel to cry for admission.

'What is this – why do you not listen to what you are told?'

'Who are you?' the woman demanded starkly. She appeared uncouth, raw to the very bones.

'Who am I? Who does not know me in these parts? I am the sister, the chief of this hospital. Listen now and do what you are told.'

'No.'

'What do you say!'

'No. My mother, that little one told me to go away. I cannot listen, I cannot go. Take me inside.'

'So you come here to lay down the law, there are no beds, there is no doctor now and no nurses to start taking in people. And how do I know you have the money to pay?'

The woman started and her jaw fell open. But she lowered her head and stubbornly came her cry again:

'My mother, take me in.'

'Come back on Monday, and find the money before you come. You cannot pass these doors without money.'

'Ah mother, you have killed me. I have no money.'

'Killed you! Here, get up and take yourself home. Enough of this sin that you come wasting my time. What is so wrong with you?'

'My time has come.'

'If every woman lay here to give birth we should need a bigger hospital than the cheese factory. Babies are born every day. Go back to your husband and let your mother-in-law deliver the child.'

'Mother!' the woman cried hoarsely and gripped the hem of Sister Scholastica's gown. 'You do not know what you are saying. I have no home. I have no husband. I will die.'

'So! Let go of me.'

'Mother, take me inside.'

'Let go, I say.'

She jerked to free herself but the thin black hand closed tighter. Leaning forward to take a firmer hold, Sister Scholastica saw with a strange shock that the woman was young and her face well shaped. From her hoarse cries, the huddle of her form and the stark, terrible way she spoke she had seemed aged. She was a mere girl – a slut. One more firm wrench loosened the gown from her grip. Sister Scholastica stepped back to close the door.

'Keep yourself out of trouble,' she said, trembling with indignation, 'and you will not come troubling others.'

Dr du Plessis walked to the hospital earlier than usual for a Sunday. The sun had not risen. The sky was cloudless, dove-coloured, shading towards the horizon into soft wonderful

layers of heliotrope and rose and only to the east beyond
the river warmed to glowing orange. All still and cold; the
dust blown clean from the path and the black burnt stubble
of a fire-brake tinged with sparkling frost. Smoke was going
up from the dreary location and on the slope facing it was
the brick and red iron building of the hospital against a line
of gum trees. She tried to look at everything freshly, not to
become stale or soured. It was one of her self-made rules to
carry the war against routine and monotony. In the greater
beauty of this cold, calm morning was the hand of the
Creator, and in the ugliness and imperfection near-by the
hand of man. No, that was not a satisfactory explanation.
The world in all its glory as also in its squalor was single,
unified and indivisible. Only in one's own heart did the
divisions exist – between dream and action; inexpressible
yearnings for joy and love and success against the nullity
and ruin of experience. Failure – failure of one's own per-
sonality, of inner hopes. Surely it was not wrong to admit
defeat in a task beyond one's given strength.

She longed to merge her feelings into the wonders of the
sky's beauty as Eve must have done watching the miracle of
dawn over Eden. Eve without responsibility and without
guilt. If any of the location dwellers or hospital staff had
seen their new doctor then they would have puzzled and
perhaps been abashed at the sad smile lighting up her tired
face and the fragility in those eyes that fascinated them with
their dauntlessness.

Magdalena had a swift insight of impending failure. She
could not be charged as yet with defeat even by her most
critical self. But the path she was treading was the wrong
one; she had chosen the wrong method and unless she could
change direction rapidly and efficiently it must be a matter

merely of time before she asked Dr Graham to be relieved of her post. Most hurtful to her passionate and impatient spirit was the thought that her own actions were not wrong, though they were producing the wrong results. Subtly, the whole staff were becoming demoralised, sapped of whatever will they had. She had wanted them to emulate her, she wanted to strike from them the flash of pride, of independence or even resistance, but instead she had produced a curious and baffling negation. They had surrendered to her and thrown on her their whole weight. She had to carry them all as well as herself. What if this staggering result had been produced by her own pride? Racial pride as a white woman, an Afrikaner; pride in her 'civilisation'. And instead of spouting it like Dr Graham's smart platform speaker, had she not set out to dazzle the Zulus with a display of medical virtuosity? If the alternative were not in old 'Weaver-bird's' inefficiency and 'Kafir psychology', where should she seek it? In the pity, the humanity of relationships between man and man, woman and woman, Dr Graham would say. To achieve it was another matter. The little nurse-aid who had taken her hand that night loved her as certainly as eyes could speak. She would die for her, she would lie down meekly and be trodden under her feet. But that was not the relationship she wanted. It cloyed the heart, a sweet but lulling drug.

She reached the hospital hoping no new patients would be clamouring outside that morning. But she saw one already, under a blanket not far from the main doors, simply a shape half propped against the wall and nothing visible save a pair of bare feet. The doctor paused before going in and looked again. Unusual and eerie, that figure alone and utterly quiet and unmoving as death. God! she thought, is this a death on our threshold? She went over and was on one knee beside the figure. The feet were ice-cold. The face she uncovered from the blanket was of a young woman, shapely and elongated like the class of 'beautiful' dancing-masks of the more northern tribes, but wasted and sunken-eyed. She was unconscious, perhaps asleep or comatose, and her lips grained with a little dry blood. Magdalena was covering her with the blanket again when she opened her eyes.

'What is your name?'

'Marta.'

'Wait a little, Marta, we will take you in. How long have you waited?'

'How long. . . .' She closed her eyes. 'I came here in the dark, is the sun rising?'

'Yes, it is rising. We will take you in now.'

'No, she will not let me in.'

'Who are you talking about?'

After a pause the young woman answered huskily. 'She has killed me, the chief sister . . . I had no money, she closed the door, she shut me out to die.'

'Wait, I will come back quickly.'

'No, stay with me, come nearer that I can see you. I am dying. . . .'

Magdalena fled for the door. In a minute she had the duty nurse and the floor-scrubber hurrying to bring in the woman. The nurse returned at once.

'There is a baby too,' she said, handing Magdalena a wretched little bundle.

The mother was put in an emergency stretcher in the aisle between the beds; a cot was rushed in with an oxygen-tent. Then Sister Scholastica appeared at the ward door and glanced at her superior, grey with alarm. She recovered herself and quickly came forward.

'Serious?' she inquired in a professionally low voice.

'Yes, very serious,' the doctor answered.

At the end of two hours' ceaseless effort to save the flickering lives Dr Magdalena found herself alone for a moment in the office. The sun was striking brightly in at the windows and the day warming up. She felt calm enough now to face Sister Scholastica with the responsibility for what she had done. The sister came in, completely self-possessed.

'I am afraid the baby is dead,' she began and was taken aback that the doctor said nothing but fixed on her a frightening look.

'Maybe it is just as well,' and she paused again at the fury rising in the other woman's expression.

'I mean, Doctor, the child is coloured – its father is a whiteman.'

'And so it is better dead?'

'I did not mean that, but – but for the poor little thing's own sake. It would be brought into a life of misery, misery and shame.'

'Do you know why it died?'

'No, Doctor, but I think you will agree it was already gone when it was brought in, most likely stillborn. It has shown no sign of life.'

'It died because you killed it, Sister Scholastica. You refused to admit the mother last night.'

'Me?' She laid a hand on her violently-heaving bosom.

'You found she could not pay. That is true, is it not?'

'True, Doctor. It is in the hospital rules – patients must pay.'

'Is it in the rules that a patient must pay with her life,

and her child's life, because she has no money?'

'You did not tell me to break the rules, Doctor,' she almost wailed.

They stood facing each other in silence. And then with a little snicker Sister Scholastica began to sob. 'Oh, I have done wrong, I have sinned. I am bad, useless. I know you think I am bad. . . .'

After a while she took out a handkerchief and dried her eyes.

'It does not matter what I think, but what you think about yourself,' Magdalena said. 'I am leaving for the city now this minute, and I shall be away two days. The patient, Marta, will be in your charge, do you understand? I am leaving her to you. I trust you with her life.'

'Oh, my God.'

'I shall report to Dr Graham.'

'Oh, God help me! What will you tell him?'

'I will tell him about you.'

'Oh Doctor Magdalena, have pity on me. If they turn me out what will I do? Must I be a servant in the kitchen, are they going to make me live down in the location in a pondok?'

'Go now and attend to the patient.'

'Oh, my mother!' Tears streamed from her eyes again and she went with her head bowed in the proud veil, wringing her hands.

Sister Scholastica felt at first an overpowering hatred for the doctor. Bustling from end to end of the hospital and returning incessantly to the bed of Marta, she threw off a sense of demoniacal energy. The nurses and aids and the ordinary labourers furtively got out of her way. There were no smiles that Sunday, and at night when Sister Scholastica

realised Marta's worst time of reaction from the shock and
exposure was nearing, an atmosphere of crisis spread even
to the male ward. She did not sleep, she drove herself all
night and all day and far into the next night. In her mind
unceasingly was the face of the doctor, her blue eyes mocking and lips curled in a smile of derision. And overlaying it
somehow until the two faces partook of a single image was
the elongated calm mask of the patient Marta. Standing in
the doorway and feeling nothing but the ache in her legs
and feet, she heard a man's voice say quietly: 'Look at the
woman! She is our life. How strong—better than the
doctor.'

She did not turn but went slowly, for the first time, to her
room. It was untrue. How could they compare her to Magdalena whom she hated? No, no, no. For a long time she sat
holding her face in her hands. No, that was untrue too. She
could look into the depths of her heart and find no trace of
hate there. The blue eyes no longer mocked her, they had
simply faded and no matter how she tried she could not re-
call Magdalena's face to her memory. She was longing for
the little doctor to walk in her gentle manner down the
ward and give her a nod of approval. She was strong and
proud enough to go her own way, if it came to that, yet she
craved the gift of courage from that nod.

Back in the ward, she took Marta's temperature and
counted her pulse, checking the record of the duty nurse.
The girl smiled at her.

'I am better, mother,' she said and fell asleep again. She
did not ask for her baby.

Marta was discharged completely recovered. She went
out silently one morning early in her rags which had been

washed and patched together. The blanket, also washed and showing its bright red to advantage, was drawn closely round her shoulders. Her eyes had come back to life, exceptionally large and pointed and shy as an animal's. With her long, slender face and small mouth and a single band of blue beads round her brow she looked like a slim, hieratic figure out of an unknown past. She went quickly and did not look back, and before the sister rose or the doctor arrived she was gone. Not a word had she uttered to them of farewell or thanks.

But Marta returned a week later, still shy-eyed, though a little fuller in the face. She carried under her arm a brown hen. Quietly she sat waiting on the kitchen doorstep with the bird and gazed intently at its bright jewel-like eye.

Sister Scholastica came out smiling and friendly. The girl stood up swiftly and held out the bird to her.

'Thank you, my child,' the sister said, touched. 'We wondered what had become of you. Is this for me?'

'No,' Marta burst out.

'Ah.' She was taken aback. 'Is it then to pay for the hospital?'

'No.' The girl seemed in a rising panic. 'No – it is for my doctor.'

She turned and hurried off and Sister Scholastica, still holding the fowl, followed her slim back until she was hidden by the gum trees. Then she untied the bird's legs and let it go in the yard. She was shocked and hurt beyond measure, and above all by the truth and justice of Marta's act. Unexpectedly she had come back to show her gratitude, and she knew to whom she owed it. Perhaps, the sister considered painfully, it was the best thing that had ever happened to her, since she had sinned. She thought of the mystery of the wild, shy girl who had lost her half-white baby. They would never know, and it was better not to inquire about her. No other inquiry was being made either. She was thankful to Dr Magdalena for that. When they were together again in the ward she must tell her about Marta's unexpected gift.

They did not meet until late afternoon. Magdalena was unhurried, and altogether she had an air of being more at ease. After some violent rocking the hospital was like a boat coming into smoother water.

'Did you know, Doctor, that Marta came back?' she said.

'Oh, indeed. And you talked to her – how is she?'

'Very much better, Doctor. She came to say thank you and she brought a present out of gratitude, a live hen.'

'She was so poor! It is one little thing like that which makes years of hard work suddenly worthwhile. I am so glad for your sake, and proud.'

'For my sake . . .' Sister Scholastica began, confused. But the doctor was looking at her, a smile turning the corners of her mouth, and she nodded with approval.

The next minute they began their round of the ward and she never really told the doctor about Marta's gift. She had just missed her chance.